Mystery at McGeehan Ranch

Mystery at McGeehan Ranch

by
Sandy Dengler

MOODY PRESS
CHICAGO

© 1982 by
THE MOODY BIBLE INSTITUTE
OF CHICAGO

Library of Congress Cataloging in Publication Data

Dengler, Sandy
  Mystery at McGeehan ranch.

  Summary: When fourteen-year-old Carrie is accused
of theft at the ranch, her friend Daniel decides to trap
the real thief.

  [1. Mystery and detective stories. 2. Ranch life—
Fiction. 3. Christian life—Fiction]
I. Title.
PZ7.D4146My   [Fic]   81-18694
ISBN 0-8024-2972-6   AACR2

Printed in the United States of America

Contents

1

The Pearl Necklace

Silent morning desert stretched away in all directions. The sky glowed clear blue, distant hills shimmered lavender, silvery incienso bushes crowned themselves with yellow daisy-like flowers. Daniel rarely noticed flowers and nice weather, but the weather had just turned fine after a week of solid, morbidly cold spring rain. You couldn't help but notice.

He slapped Roller's ribs with his heels and drew his knees up. Roller sighed, let his nose drop low, and started forward down the steep hillside. Even with his knees up, Daniel hurt. Roller was so painfully bony, his backbone so sharp, there was no way to straddle him comfortably.

A wild whoop came echoing out of the canyon beside them. Daniel pulled Roller up and swung him broadside of the hill. He listened. Other cowboy voices yelled. Hooves and rattling stones clattered toward him down the canyon.

From somewhere among mesquites Wahoo's voice called, "Turn 'm, Dan!"

Daniel forgot instantly the discomfort of riding Roller bareback. He pushed the little horse forward as the first of a bunch of spook-eyed longhorns came popping out of the brush. A big, brindled blue-gray cow skidded to a stop to stare at him. Her new calf and two other cows appeared beside her. They milled about a moment, confused.

Daniel shook his coiled rope out to the side and pretended he was about to throw a loop. Rope-wise, the brindled cow turned and bolted back the way she had come. Her calf followed stiff-legged, its tail sticking straight up.

It was a pure bluff—Daniel could not rope a cow if he wanted to. He had no saddle and therefore nothing to tie the rope to. He saw Wahoo's tall hat moving among bushes along the wash. He heard a rope whistle.

Wahoo's voice called, "Turn 'm again, Dan!"

The brindled bossy charged out of the brush and wagged her horns at Daniel. He shook his rope. She hesitated. He could see Wahoo and the others just upcanyon, faded hats and jackets flitting in and out of the weedy bushes.

It was all those cowboys or plain old Daniel. The cow made her choice. She put her head low and started trotting right toward him. He shook his rope violently, but she would not be fooled. Yet Wahoo had said to turn her. In desperation Daniel threw his loop at her head.

A perfect throw! The rope settled over her horns and dropped around her neck. But now what? She broke into a choppy run and clattered past him. He had no way to stop her, no way to slow her down, no place to dally his end of the rope. He was considering that he might somehow brace himself against Roller if he could get Roller turned around just so, when she reached the end of the rope and kept running.

Daniel knew he really ought to let go, but the rope was a loan from Wahoo. He must not lose it. His arm yanked nearly out of joint. His head snapped back as he shot forward—off Roller, over a low bush, and out across the hard gravel wash. He managed to grab the rope in both hands as the cow dragged him along.

He realized vaguely that one or more cows were running alongside him on the left and a horse bucketed along on his right. An incienso bush—a pretty little thing—came at him very fast. He smashed into it. His hands caught fire as the rope disappeared. Wahoo's rope was gone forever!

Daniel flopped over on his back and stared at the clear blue awhile. He had lost not only Wahoo's rope but the cows as well. He was a dirt farmer. He had grown up a farmer, and he would always be a stupid, dirty old farmer. He would never earn the right to be called a cowboy. Tears trickled down each side of his face and made puddles in his ears.

"Glory, look at his hands!" Wahoo's face blocked out the blue sky above him.

Wahoo was no more than eighteen, but he was everything Daniel had always wanted to be and never would be. With a practiced flick of his rope Wahoo could catch up a cow's hind legs every throw. He could flank a calf down faster than eyes could watch. He was not much bigger than Daniel (in fact, he was small for his age), and yet he carried a huge, ungainly pistol at his side. Daniel's mother did not believe in guns.

Daniel turned his eyes away, too embarrassed to apologize. Wahoo grabbed his wrists and yanked. Daniel jerked to his feet more or less in spite of himself.

"What a mess!" Wahoo grinned. "What a ring-tailed, howling mess! You look like the first time I lit in a cactus patch!"

Daniel stared at the insides of his hands. Both were raw, the skin torn away in some places and rubbed off in others. The rips and burns oozed bloody, watery fluid. No wonder they hurt!

A shadow fell across his face as Mr. Frazier stepped in front of him. Mr. Frazier was the new ranch foreman, and now he, too, would know that Daniel was just a bumbling little old dirt farmer.

"Tore yourself up proper, boy. Looks like you won't be riding for a while."

Daniel's consternation quenched his embarrassment. "They aren't so bad, sir! Really! I can still ride Roller. He handles easy anyway. And I'm sorry your cows got away." He turned to Wahoo. "And I'm sorry I lost your rope."

"Who says?" Wahoo gestured off down the wash. "That stupid stunt of yours slowed her up so much we managed to drop a rope on the whole swarmy bunch."

Mr. Frazier nodded. "Fair throw you made. Only next time make sure you have something solid to anchor onto. Like a saddle." His voice was trying to be mean, but his eyes twinkled. Daniel did not know which to believe.

The foreman was right. Daniel's hands would be useless for days. No riding, no wagon-driving, not even wood-splitting. Mr. Frazier scooped him up and plunked him on Roller's back as though he were a four-year-old. Daniel could do nothing but sit there helpless, as Wahoo caught up Roller's reins and led him down the wash. Daniel's eyes got hot.

The week had begun so gloriously, too. Last autumn Daniel had worked corrals at Mr. McGeehan's ranch. And now Colin McGeehan had hired him for spring roundup. Here was Daniel, only fourteen years old, hired at a man's wages to do a cowboy's work. It was a dream come true—until now. With Pop dead nearly six months now, there was not a penny to spare in the Tremain house. Mom needed Daniel's wages, and he could work no more.

Daniel watched the white canvas wagon top

take shape beyond the brush and rocks ahead. The chuck wagon sat out on a warm, open hill-side. Beside it a fire slithered around lazily on glowing coals. Wonderful smells wafted on its trickle of pale blue smoke—smells of too-strong coffee, of dampened charcoal, of the slab of beef roasting on a spit.

In the shade of the wagon the camp cook stood up from peeling potatoes and wiped his hands on his apron. Daniel could not imagine his Mom letting her apron get that dirty, but then she was not a camp cook.

Wahoo called, "Got a casualty, Perfesser." His voice sounded just plain jolly.

The camp cook, called "Perfesser" by everyone on the ranch including Mr. McGeehan, ruled like a king. Even the foreman smiled and took his guff. Daniel felt terrible that this Perfesser would now see the results of his foolishness. He swung his leg over Roller's withers and slid to the ground.

Wahoo jabbed him, nudged him forward. "Show 'm, Dan."

Daniel held out his hands for inspection. Two cowboys, their forty-pound Mexican saddles slung casually over their shoulders, hung around to look. Daniel felt his cheeks flush.

The Perfesser grunted and wandered off. Wahoo began explaining loudly how Daniel tried to rope a cow bareback. He sounded proud of it!

The Perfesser came wandering back, uncorking a big brown bottle. He poured foul amber fluid all over Daniel's hands, mumbling something about the healing powers of corn whiskey. If that was whiskey, Daniel could not imagine anyone wanting to drink the stuff. And if it burned your mouth half as bad as it burned his hands—

Quite a group had gathered around by now. Daniel must be a real sideshow attraction. His cheeks burned as hot as his hands. It was remarkably quiet, too, but for the heckling.

"Seen healthier looking meat in a smokehouse."

"Better not let no cannibal see them hands, boy."

"Hope you wasn't planning to play the fiddle tonight."

"Or serenade your girlfriend."

"Don't expect much applause outta this boy."

The razzing made Daniel feel better. Cowboys only tease people they like. No one called him stupid or foolish. No one seemed angry. He regretted now only that he could not earn money for his mom. Mr. Frazier rode in among the group and swung down.

The Perfesser pointed toward a cowboy. "Turn the meat half around, Pete. He going back to the ranch, Mr. Frazier?"

The foreman nodded. "Can't help you here, can he?"

"Not likely. Better give it to 'm now then, y' s'pose?"

"Looks like we shoulda given it to him yesterday."

"Weren't finished yesterday." The Perfesser tucked his brown bottle away under the wagon seat.

Daniel looked at Wahoo's face, but the answer was not there. Mr. Frazier still had that sneaky twinkle about him.

The Perfesser pushed past Mr. Frazier and dropped a saddle at Daniel's feet. "Hit's your'n, boy. Hope you like it."

"No, sir," Daniel shook his head. "I'm afraid you made a mistake. See, Pop never owned a saddle, and I don't ei—" His voice stopped, choked off by the lump in his throat.

It was a brand new saddle, a beautiful saddle. The leather puckered just a little at the base of the fork; hammer marks showed in the iron D-rings; the cinches were braided of horsehair the color of Roller's tail. It had been handmade right here on the ranch by the men standing all around him now. He knelt down and reached out, but he dare not touch the leather and risk soiling it with his battered hands. The saddle melted to a brown blur as Daniel's eyes filled up and overflowed.

"I suppose you bums are standing here waiting for Christmas," the Perfesser thundered. "Well, until I get some more firewood and a full

14

barrel of water, nobody eats. So you better move!"

The many pairs of knees around Daniel drifted away. He sat in the loose dirt beside his new saddle and spent long minutes running the back of his hand across the cool, smooth leather.

Daniel wished he were still out with the others on roundup. His hands had coated over since yesterday with a stiff, unappetizing crust. They hurt every time he flexed his fingers. But he still could ride Roller by looping the knotted reins over his wrist. And his brand new saddle felt heavenly. How had he put up with Roller's razorback so long? Roller's pacing gait carried him under the tall, mesquite-pole archway and into the McGeehan ranch yard.

Daniel realized with a happy little tickle that Mom was here at the ranch today. She came to tutor Mr. McGeehan's daughter Bridgid on Mondays and Thursdays. (Bridgid's brother Ern would probably tutor her when he returned from the Eastern school he was attending.) This was a Thursday. Daniel could hardly wait to show Mom his saddle.

Carrie was here, too! He saw her in the distance, just coming out of the house. Carrie, Daniel had to admit, was his best friend despite the fact she was a girl. But then Daniel only knew two girls here in Arizona (not counting his three sisters, of course).

And now the second girl he knew came out. Bridgid was a year younger than Daniel and Carrie—soon-to-be thirteen—but she looked sophisticated as a queen. She was not at all like Carrie or like Daniel's sisters or like any other girl in the whole world. She was special, with milk-white skin and bouncing, coppery-red curls.

She flounced across the yard and grabbed Carrie's arm, yanking her to a stop. "I said, 'Give it back!' "

"And I said," Carrie's voice was cool and crisp, "that I didn't take it."

Bridgid shoved Carrie back a step. "Give it to me!"

Carrie pushed, and Bridgid staggered back three feet. Carrie's voice rose angrily. "You are a spoiled, useless brat with a mouth like a Galveston dockhand. I wouldn't give you the satisfaction of taking what's yours, even if I wanted to, which I don't. You don't own a solitary thing I would ever want."

Bridgid gasped. Her milky complexion turned red. She shrieked a very nasty word and lunged at Carrie. Daniel slid off Roller quickly. Bridgid might be angry, but piling into Carrie like that was pound-foolish. Carrie was a year older and a lot stronger from hard work. Besides, although Carrie never picked a fight, she sure knew how to handle herself in squabbles with her brothers.

Daniel tried to wedge himself between the

16

grappling girls. "Cut it out, you two, before Mom sees you!"

The girls turned as one, shouted, "You stay out of this!" and pushed him away. He almost lost his footing and sat down.

Daniel's mom appeared from nowhere and plunged both arms into the fray. Instantly the girls were four feet apart. *How did she do that so smoothly?*

"Bridgid, what's going on here?"

"She took the necklace with the pearl; the one I showed you this morning. She took it, and she must give it back right now!"

Carrie sighed and brushed herself off. "I did no such thing. She showed it to me after lunch, and that's the only time I ever saw it."

"I put it on my vanity, and you went in and took it! It's gone."

Carrie snorted. "If you have such wonderful expensive stuff, why don't you learn to keep track of it, *Miss* McGeehan?" She looked at Mom. "I'll go harness Caesar." She walked casually off toward the corrals.

"Bridgid, are you certain you put it on your vanity?" Mom asked.

Bridgid stamped her dainty foot. "Sure 'n ye'd side with that little snippet! Her father's courting ye! Well, she's a thief all the same, and Daddy will take care of her! And yourself as well!" She flounced those glorious copper curls and pranced off to the house.

Mom closed her eyes. "The money's wel-

come, but this tutoring job has its moments."
She smiled at Daniel. "Hope your week's going
smoother than mine. How's the—land sakes!
Whatever happened to your hands?!"

"I'll tell you about it. What was all that?"

Mom put an arm across his shoulder, and
they started walking toward the house. "Bridgid was showing off a new necklace this
morning—a solitaire pearl on a fine gold chain.
Very pretty. And—well, you heard. The last
thing Mr. McGeehan needs is something like
this."

Daniel opened his mouth to speak and
closed it again. A tall young man, a stranger,
stepped out of the house and paused on the
porch in front of them. Didn't he look
elegant—the perfect gentleman, straight out of
the fashion books! A tattersall vest peeked
from beneath his black coat. His little black
hat sat square and solid on his head. He looked
to be only a year or two older than Wahoo—
certainly less than twenty-one.

He tipped his hat to Mom. "Good afternoon,
Mrs. Tremain." He smiled toward Daniel,
bounded down off the porch, and swung
aboard a scrawny little sorrel horse. He nodded
toward Mom again and rode away.

Daniel found himself staring. "Now, who's
that?"

"Galen Sanger, a professional accountant.
Mr. McGeehan's financial records are in a terrible muddle, so he hired that young man to

18

unmuddle them." She gave Daniel a motherly nudge toward the door. "Come into the kitchen. I want to hear about those hands."

Galen Sanger's horse clattered out the gate and the young man himself skipped Daniel's mind—for the moment.

2

And Now a Spoon

The McGeehan kitchen contained more or less the same furnishings as did the Tremain kitchen—a wood stove, a table, shelves—but it did not feel the same at all. Mr. McGeehan never set foot in here. Nobody laughed around the table. Inez the cook presided here, and she considered everyone else to be a trespasser.

Daniel and Carrie sat at the table feeling like trespassers. So did Grace, Daniel's eleven-year-old sister. No one spoke. Inez served them tea because she was supposed to, but only Carrie drank any. Daniel noticed that she spooned in lots of sugar.

In the dining room beyond, Mom sat talking to Mr. McGeehan about "the problem." Daniel was sick of the problem. Bridgid had mislaid her necklace. Why did she not simply search the corners of her room? Perhaps she had found it already, but she hated Carrie so much that she did not tell anyone. Daniel scowled. He must mention that possibility to Mom.

Bridgid was capable of that sort of thing; she was vindictive, like Grace.

Daniel heard, without trying, snatches of the conversation in the next room. Mom was admitting that theft could be a very real temptation to Carrie; the girl felt bad that she was not a wage earner during these hard times. But no, Mom was quite positive Carrie's moral character was above theft and that she would never yield to such a temptation, however strong. Her voice poured as Mr. McGeehan's rumbled. No doubt Mom could talk an Eskimo into buying a coconut splitter.

Grace pouted at her teacup. "Why did Mom have to come over here on a Saturday, anyway? It's ruining the whole day."

"That sounds just like you," Daniel grumbled. "Carrie's honor is on the line, and you complain about giving up a couple hours of play time. Why didn't you bring your knitting and redeem the time, like Matt says?"

"She wanted to come today because Mr. McGeehan was all upset Thursday, and she wanted to be able to keep it civilized." Carrie peeked into her empty cup.

With a sigh Inez refilled it. She disliked the intrusion of trespassers as much as the trespassers did. Carrie dumped two heaping spoons of sugar in her cup and stirred.

Daniel was considering Carrie's sugar-in-a-bit-of-tea idea when Mom appeared at the doorway, smiling pleasantly. "Children, come."

Grace bounced up and hastened toward the door. Mom stopped her instantly with her specialty—a grip like a pipe wrench where your neck meets your shoulder. Grace walked out quietly and even remembered to thank Inez for the tea.

Outside Daniel climbed into the back of the wagon with Grace. Mom had to drive, because his hands were still too sore. He leaned in the corner against the tailgate and watched late afternoon sunshine make the hills change colors. The dirt road poured out from behind the wagon and lay in ragged curves among the hills.

Carrie and Mom were sitting on the box facing ahead, and Grace was falling asleep. It was Daniel who saw the cloud of dust on the road far behind them. "Mom! Traveling companions behind!"

Pop used to carry a shotgun under the seat, "just in case." Is it still there? Daniel groped beneath coils of spare rope and an extra singletree. There it was; he worked it free and dragged it out.

"Dan, no." Mom was twisted in her seat watching the dust.

"Just in case." Daniel broke the gun open, made sure it held two good shells, and snapped it closed. He laid it carefully by the tailgate and sat down beside it to watch.

"Suppose it's Indians?" Carrie's experience with the Apache band was still fresh in her memory. Her face was white.

Daniel saw a bowler hat bob in the distance. "Looks Irish more than Indian. Bet it's Mr. McGeehan. Did one of us forget something?"

Mom dragged Caesar and Cleopatra to a stop and set the brake. It was Mr. McGeehan all right. He came thundering over the hill with his coattails flying. Beside the wagon he hauled his little horse in so fiercely that it squealed as it sat down on its haunches.

He stared at Carrie with a scowl that would strike terror into a Barbary pirate. "The silver sugar shell is missing!"

Daniel wanted to think a moment. What was a shell? And why was Mr. McGeehan addressing Carrie with the problem?

No one had that moment to think. *"Well?"*

Mom's voice cut like ice. "Mr. McGeehan, this may be Arizona Territory; but the year is 1883, and the world at large is now civilized. I invite you to join the times and speak with a civil tongue."

He melted a bit, only a bit, and turned his eyes to her. "Inez claims it was on the table when the children were in the kitchen. An heirloom it is, from the auld country, and worth a pretty penny."

"S'cuse me," said Daniel. "What's a sugar shell?"

Mom's eyes never left Colin McGeehan.

24

"The spoon out of the sugar bowl."

Daniel shook his head. "It was right there, sticking out of the sugar. We didn't even use it. The only one who put sugar in anything was Car—" The world stopped cold. His head whipped around to stare at her.

"I didn't!" Her eyes turned, wild and frightened, to Mom. "I didn't!"

Mom nodded and faced Mr. McGeehan. Her shoulders were back square and she looked boiling mad—the boilingest Daniel had ever seen her. "Sir, you have insulted not only these children and me but my husband's good name as well. If your housekeeper mislaid a spoon that's your problem and hers. We will be at our home by Tubac when you choose to make an apology." She turned and clucked to the horses, releasing the brake with a vengeance. The wagon lurched forward.

Mr. McGeehan's horse danced in place a few moments. Then he wrenched its head around cruelly and spurred it away, up and over the hill and out of sight.

That was not just Mr. McGeehan disappearing over the hill. It was also Daniel's job as a cowboy, Mom's job as a tutor, and Bridgid. Daniel would never see Bridgid again. Since the death of Carrie's mother and Daniel's father, the Tremains and the Carsons associated closely, combining their resources to make ends meet. It was almost like a single double-big family, and Bridgid recognized that too. If one Carson was a thief, the whole pack must be thieves. She would never speak to him again.

Daniel rode home in a black cloud.

3

A Tie Tack, Too

Daniel sat sprawled in his chair at the table and compared Mom's kitchen here with the McGeehans—that one so cold; this one so warm and friendly. Grace snapped orders like the emperor of Japan as she directed the younger children in setting the table. Mom and Carrie chatted as they cooked. Everything blended comfortably.

Carrie's older brother Matt paused in the doorway drying his hands. He tossed the towel out of sight toward the outdoor washstand and came over to plop in the chair next to Daniel. "Finally met that Galen Sanger. He's a choirmaster."

"He's not much older than you. What's he doing leading choirs?"

"Says he's been doing it nearly three years. In fact, apparently he started it—the choir. He wasn't speaking boastfully, understand. But I also learned he was considering the ministry before he got into accounting."

How could a person that young make a career change, let alone set upon a career? Daniel was beginning to feel a little childish. All he thought about was being a cowboy. *But what is wrong with being a cowboy?*

Mom was asking Matt, "How'd the sermon go today?"

"Very well, with the Lord's blessing. Mrs. Carson, I really love this circuit preaching— here, Tubac at mid-morning, Augustine Ranch at noon. I got some excellent responses to the message today, too."

"Wonderful."

Now Daniel felt really left out of life. Matt at sixteen was all launched on a career, Galen Sanger was what the world calls a *success*, and Daniel could not even be a good cowboy.

"What was your topic?" Mom set a steamed pudding on the table.

"Temptation. Why God uses it, how we avoid it, and what we do when we can't avoid it."

Carrie's father popped in through the door so suddenly that Daniel jumped. He dragged his dusty hat off as Carrie and her little brothers ran to him for a hug. The Tremain girls—all three of them—did, too.

Mom turned away from the stove to give Mr. Carson the kind of bright smile she once gave only to Pop. "Glad you made it, Hank. I was afraid you'd be detained and miss dinner."

"Not a chance! I'll go wash up. Just be a

minute." He dropped his hat on the peg by the door—the peg where Pop used to put his—and started outside. He stopped in the doorway. "Hallo."

Llorón, Daniel's hound, let loose his "Someone's coming!" howl. Daniel reached the door before his mom did.

Mr. McGeehan dismounted by the door and threw his reins over the porch rail. Llorón moved in closer to sniff. The rancher leaned over and rubbed the bony hound head.

Mr. Carson stepped down off the porch. "Hank Carson, Carrie's father."

"Ah! The very man I wish to see." The Irishman extended his hand. "Colin McGeehan, at your service."

"What can we do for you?" Mr. Carson's voice suggested that there was not a solitary thing he wanted to do for him. Daniel remembered well how angry he had become when Mom and Carrie told him about "the problem."

"I've come to make an apology. Mrs. Tremain, Inez found the sugar shell down under the cabinets in a corner. Highly curious, but there it was. I offer no excuses, and I do apologize."

"But not about the necklace."

"I'm sure me daughter'll come across it in good time." Mr. McGeehan nodded toward Carrie. "I'm sorry, lass. And Mr. Carson, 'twas a good pleasure meeting ye." He glanced at

Daniel. "I trust ye'll be coming back to work shortly, lad. We need ye."

"Thank you, sir! Yes, sir!" Daniel could not hide his elation.

Mom and Mr. Carson invited Mr. McGeehan to dinner, but he declined with profuse thanks. Finally he mounted to leave. The afternoon sun flashed green fire at his throat. His tie was tacked down by a pin of some sort set with a gleaming green jewel. Daniel did not doubt a moment that it was a genuine emerald. Mr. McGeehan was brusque and gentle by whim, but never was he phony.

Why should that silver spoon end up under a cabinet? No matter. Carrie was cleared. Well, almost. And Daniel could hardly wait to be back on the job again; sitting in his new saddle, driving cattle, and being a cowboy.

Cowboys arrange themselves in clusters. Daniel scraped the last of his beans off his tin plate and contemplated that latest-learned fact about cowboys. Closest to the campfire were the older men—Mr. Frazier and the fellows whose bellies bulged out over their belts. Off to themselves were five young men who liked to pal around together. They laughed a lot and worked as little as possible, it seemed to Daniel. They were Wahoo's age, but for some reason Wahoo never much associated with them. Tonight he made a group all by himself. He was wedged against the trunk of a mesquite, apart from fire and companionship, in a tiny space that permitted only one person.

That left Daniel by himself. The young cowboys (but apparently not Wahoo) considered him a little kid. And he certainly was not one of the older men.

In the draw below camp, some cow murmured to another cow and received a rumbling reply. The last bright edge of sun disappeared behind the hills. The sky, once blue, faded from white to yellow within moments. Daniel flopped back, using his saddle as a sort of bony pillow, to watch the stars come out.

"Visitor." A lookout's distant voice brought Daniel up to sitting instantly. Mr. Frazier stood up.

Moments later a little gray horse materialized in the waning light. Her rider was one of the older group, but not a cowboy. His belly lapped out over his belt buckle. He had buttoned his black coat up close around his neck and had pulled his spotted and stained old hat around his ears. Like most men in Indian country he carried a pistol on his leg and a carbine on his saddle. He rode directly into the circle of firelight and slowly, stiffly climbed off his mare. A star-shaped badge on his coat caught the orange fire glow.

The young cowboys turned instantly silent and glanced at one another nervously.

Mr. Frazier extended a hand. "Otis Frazier."

"Hosea Cadder. Pleezdameetcha." The visitor shook hands quickly and squatted down as close to the fire as he could get. He toasted his hands, rubbing them together. " 'Spected to get here two hours ago. Might just stay over, if you don't mind."

"Not atall. Perfesser's fixing you a plate. What can we do ya for?" Mr. Frazier sat down in his usual place.

"I'm sheriff's deputy and the Tubac constable—sort of a combination position. Investigating a matter, and I got some questions for a young feller named Daniel, if he be about. Daniel Tremain."

Every eye in camp turned to Daniel. Why in the world would this man want to speak to him? The tallest of the young cowboys, Wick somebody, mumbled a remark and the others laughed.

Mr. Cadder stood up, accepted a heaping tin plate with thanks, and walked over to Daniel. He wiggled a finger, and the two of them walked out into the gathering darkness.

Mr. Cadder sat down and balanced his plate on his knee. Daniel sat down beside him. "So you're Daniel Tremain. Smaller'n I expected. Hear you got a new saddle."

"Yes, sir."

Mr. Cadder's eyes turned on him suddenly, dark and suspicious. "And what'd you buy it with? Where'd you get the money?"

"Didn't, sir. It was given to me."

"By who?" His voice made Daniel feel guilty.

"The fellows here. The cowboys. They made it."

"Folks buy anything new lately? Your ma and that Carson?"

"Not that I know of. But I haven't been home for a couple days."

"Hm." Mr. Cadder turned his attention to his plate. He mouthed his beans awhile. The spoon clanked against the tin. "How well do you know this Carrie Carson?"

"She's my best friend."

Mr. Cadder stared at him. "Boy your age got a girl friend?"

"Not a girl friend. I said my *best* friend."

"There's a difference?"

"Far as I'm concerned, sir."

Was Mr. Cadder smiling a little? Daniel could not tell. The constable/deputy chewed some more. He seemed to be chewing thoughts more than beans. "Answer me this. The truth. Has this Carrie ever done anything illegal that you know of?"

"Never. You mean like steal a necklace?"

"Or a silver spoon or a—"

"They found the spoon, sir. It was under some cabinets, Mr. McGeehan said." Daniel wished he could see Mr. Cadder's face, but it was getting too dark.

"It's gone again. Also some gold-rimmed glasses—little glasses—pince-nez. And an

33

emerald tie tack."

"I know for a fact Carrie would never take one thing, let alone all those things."

"How about you?"

"Me neither. Besides, I haven't been around there."

"You were around there enough. The glasses could've been taken any time. In fact, your Carrie delivered a message out to the ranch the same day that Sanger boy noticed them missing. And the tie tack disappeared the day Mr. McGeehan visited your farm, and you and Carrie were both there."

"Big green emerald, right? Mr. McGeehan was still wearing his tie tack when he left our farm, sir. I remember."

Mr. Cadder no doubt borrowed his tone of voice from the Spanish Inquisition. Daniel felt condemned. "Now what would a boy your age be doing noticing a tie tack?"

"I probably wouldn't, but the sun caught it just right."

Mr. Cadder was staring at him, but probably the man could see no better than Daniel could. "You deny knowing anything about this."

"Yes, sir. Nor having any part in it, either."

The spoon scraped across the tin plate. Mr. Cadder stood up suddenly, so Daniel followed, uncertain.

They walked back to the fire and Mr. Cadder squatted down again close to the coals. Daniel assumed the questioning must be over with.

He stretched out again to watch stars and thought about Carrie. Might she really have yielded to temptation? Surely not. She, like Daniel (in fact, like both the Carson and Tremain families), was a servant of Jesus Christ. Christians do not steal.

Do they?

4

Wahoo Comes to Grief

Seventy cows trailed out across the broad, open basin, their heads and dewlaps wagging as they walked. Daniel noticed a marked tendency in cows to drag their feet. He noticed further that they were prone to drag their feet most where the ground was dustiest and when Daniel was at the rear of the herd.

Daniel rode at the rear of the herd now. "Riding drag," it was called. You push the cows along from behind and urge on stragglers. You also get the worst of the dust. He tied his bandanna over his nose and mouth, bandit style, but the dust still made him sneeze and cough. It made his teeth gritty. It put hard, black "sleepers" in the corners of his eyes. It coated his old horse and his new saddle, his hair, his clothes. It stuck to his skin and made him feel sticky.

On the far periphery of this ambling herd an old cow suddenly thrust her head and horns sideways at a steer. The steer lunged aside and trotted out across the open flat. Wahoo separated from the trailing cowboys and spurred his horse off in pursuit. Daniel watched admiringly. Wahoo gauged the steer's reactions perfectly and flicked his romal only once. The steer veered back and lost itself in the bawling, plodding bunch. Wahoo was a grand cowboy. Why didn't the others ever talk to him or include him in their joking and roughhousing?

They left the broad flats behind and began winding through the canyons that would bring them home to the ranch. Mr. Frazier and the older men rode on ahead. They would reach the ranch in an hour or less and would have bathed and shaved by the time the cows came in. It was a privilege of seniority.

Wick took the lead, and Wahoo fell in beside Daniel at the rear. Contrary left his place midway and rode ahead to tell Wick a joke. Contrary knew more jokes than Matt knew Bible verses. Daniel had heard his true name was Manuel Contreres; but Wick never called anyone by his proper name. *What is Wick a nickname for?* Daniel wondered.

Daniel yipped at a laggard calf. "Wahoo, how come we're getting so strung out?"

"Cause them ya-hoos up ahead aren't paying attention. We should be keeping this bunch a lot tighter, or we're gonna have cows all over Aunt Maude's pea patch. Shake your rope loose, and we'll push 'm a little harder back here."

Daniel did so, delighted. He and Wahoo were

operating as a team. It gave him an elegant feeling of pride.

Wahoo had his half of the stragglers jogging. Daniel's half were harder to convince. Wahoo called, "Done some eavesdropping last night."

"You mean when Mr. Cadder was talking to me?"

"Yeah. I was curious. You know, I don't think that little Carson girl would do such a thing. She seems pretty straight-forward—looks you right in the eye. In fact, she's gonna be a mighty fine lady in a couple years."

"I think so, too. But that's a lot of things missing to just chalk it off to carelessness."

"How about the Gladsinger?"

"Who?"

"That choirmaster, that Galen Sanger."

The Gladsinger! What a perfect name for that strange young man! "What about him?"

"Maybe he's the thief."

"Nah. He's a good church person."

Wahoo rode in closer, lowered his voice. "You told me that whether you go to church, or what church it is, has nothing to do with the condition of your heart. You said it's only how you relate to Jesus Christ."

"That's true. You have to know Jesus personally and obey Him. But—"

"So what if the Gladsinger goes to church? Ever ask him about his relationship to Jesus?"

"Never talked to him, really. Matt did a little.

And Carrie seems impressed that he's a true Christian." Daniel rode in silence awhile, thinking. The rash of thefts (if thefts they were) and the Gladsinger all arrived about the same time. Could it be?

From up front Wick called, "What's the hurry back there?"

Wahoo shouted through the dust, "Bunch 'm up! They're too strung out."

"Who's running this show, anyway?"

"You won't have a show to run if any little thing spooks 'm!"

The cowboys up ahead called to each other. Daniel heard Wick laugh.

Wahoo didn't seem to mind. "Just keep pushing 'm," he said pleasantly.

Like an ungainly, disjointed caterpillar, the loose herd threaded up between close and crumbly canyon walls. The walls opened wider; their sharp lips softened into gently curving hillsides splotched with creosote bushes. Daniel's leg brushed now and then against a bush. Crackly dry leaves found their way down inside his socks.

Ahead and beyond the line of wagging horns the ground suddenly exploded. A mule deer doe jumped to her feet and bounded away up the hill. Almost under the cattle's hooves her twin fawns leaped from invisibility to airborne and spronged off in two other directions.

Instantly Daniel was engulfed in horns and dusty, hairy backs. Cows bolted in all

40

directions—snorting, bugling, thundering. Daniel knew without being told that he must swing wide and try to bring the scattering strays back together. On the other side of the churning confusion Wahoo was leaning forward on his horse, riding straight up the steep shoulder of the wash. Daniel paused, his attention diverted from the cattle to Wahoo. How that boy could ride!

Wahoo whooped and slapped his reata down across a crooked-horned steer. The flustered beast bawled and ran obediently back down to the main bunch. Wahoo's horse clawed across the side of the hill, hot in pursuit of a cow with this year's calf. The cow stumbled, lurched, then regained her footing.

As Daniel watched from too far away, Wahoo's horse squealed and pitched forward among the rocks. Its hindquarters poised high in the air, writhing, for one long moment, then dropped. The horse slammed down across the rocks, twisted and rolled down the steep hillside, and finally thudded into the loose sand of the wash. Somewhere under that thousand pounds of squirming, struggling horse lay Wahoo.

Daniel sat all scrunched up on his upper bunk, his legs drawn up, his chin resting on his knees. The warm, smoky air made him sleepy. Although four coal oil lamps made the bunkhouse brighter than usual for nighttime,

Daniel's bunk was always dark.

Mr. McGeehan came stomping in the door. He squatted down beside the lower bunk across from Daniel's. "And how's he doing, Mrs. Tremain?"

Mom sat up straight and smiled. "Pretty well, I believe. Miraculous that he wasn't killed. Wahoo, can you think of anything we might have missed?"

Wahoo's voice sounded much stronger now than it did an hour ago. "Everything's all right, I think. Thank you, ma'am."

Mr. McGeehan nodded, his bushy head barely visible. "We're grateful to ye, madam, for coming so far out here to help this lad. And ye know y'r business. Daniel was right in fetching ye."

"I'm hardly a doctor, Mr. McGeehan. I wish there were a doctor about. Back injuries are dangerous."

"Ye said he pulled some muscles? Nothing broken?"

"It seems so. All the same, Wahoo, you stay down and quiet, just in case."

"He will!" Mr. McGeehan stood up. "Would ye join us at the house for a bit of tea, madam?"

"I can certainly use a bit of tea. Thank you." Mom stood up and Mr. McGeehan held the door for her. She didn't even say anything to Daniel as she left. She would be returning later, of course, but still—.

Daniel felt left out—detached somehow. He thought of their home in Texas a year ago. It had been a complete home, with Mom and Pop and his sisters and him. He was only now beginning to realize how encompassing and comforting that home had felt. There was no home like that any more. Pop was gone and could not be replaced. Mom came and went, picking up odd jobs like sewing and tutoring. The Carson family had invaded—not intentionally, of course. The little adobe house meant only for Tremains was exploding under the added pressure of the Carson children.

Besides, Daniel missed Chet. Chet was the same age as Wahoo and Wick and his pals; in fact, Contrary was younger. None of them save Wahoo could measure up to strong, knowledgeable, enthusiastic Chet Hollis. But Chet was still in Texas, along with all the old memories and the comfort.

"Hey, Dan?"

Daniel jumped down and plunked himself on the edge of Wahoo's bunk, where Mom had been sitting moments before.

"I really like your mother. She's gentle but she's firm. And she's not sticky, you know?"

"Sticky?"

"My Aunt Edith was sticky. You got a bloody nose or something else ordinary and she swarmed all over you, whining, 'Oh, you poor little dear!' Sappy."

"Yeah. Mom doesn't embarrass you."

43

"That's it. And she laced up this wrenched knee real fine. It hurts, but not near as much. How many cows did Wick manage to save together?"

"I didn't notice. Maybe twenty-five or thirty. I lost interest in cows. I had enough trouble getting your horse to climb off you."

"Did they, uh—?"

Daniel considered a moment. It was Wahoo's horse, and he ought to know, even if it was bad news. "They didn't. I did. With your gun. It had a broken leg; near fore. There was no saving it. I'm sorry."

"Don't apologize for shooting him if his leg was broke." Wahoo stared awhile at the bottom of the bunk above his. "Hit was a good horse. Real good horse."

Somehow Daniel held Wick responsible, though he could not say just why. "Can I get you something?"

"No." Wahoo looked at Daniel. "Yeah. Last fall when you told me about Jesus and I agreed to turn myself over to Him, you said I should read the Bible. Well, I don't have one. But here I am laid up for who knows how long with lots of time to read. Suppose you could find me a Bible?"

Daniel hopped up so quickly that he clunked his head on the bunk above. "I sure could!" He climbed to his own bed and dug into the folds of his extra quilt. It took a moment to find his Bible. "Here. Use mine." He climbed down and handed it to Wahoo.

The boy scowled. "What was it doing tucked away in there?"

Daniel sat down again. "Uh, not much time, y'know."

"Not much guts, right? Afraid Wick or somebody'll laugh at you if they see you reading a Bible."

"Not exactly—"

"Ashamed of it, right? Ever tell Wick about Jesus?"

"Sort of, once."

"Well, just remember. If you'd kept your mouth shut to me I'd be going to hell on a greased pole now." Wahoo laid the book beside him. "Just like they're doing. Thanks for the Bible."

"Sure." Daniel was happy that lamplight does not show colors well. He felt his ears getting hot and, no doubt, red.

"Any cattle in the Bible?"

"Not many. Lotsa sheep."

"Sheep." Wahoo snuffed.

Daniel knew what Wahoo thought of sheep. "Hey, there's one place. Interesting. They hitch up these mother cows, see, and pen their calves up at home." Daniel dragged the Bible into his lap and fumbled through pages. He finally found it in chapter 6 of First Samuel. "Here. The cows' calves are home bawling, but the cows head straight as an arrow up the road to Israel—leave the calves behind. It's a miracle, really. The cows actually wanted to go home."

Wahoo brightened. "I'll read it tomorrow. Kinda tired now."

"Me too. Long day."

"Wasn't it, though!"

One of the oil lamps sputtered, nearly dry. Daniel walked over and blew it out. A long day indeed. Sitting beside Wahoo for years (actually, it was only a few hours) until Mr. Frazier got there; destroying Wahoo's horse and *then* trying to salvage the saddle (he should have unsaddled it before he shot it); waiting for Mom while Wahoo lay stiff and white, unable to breathe well; and through it all, Wick's insolent "So what?" attitude. And now it was nearly midnight.

Daniel crawled up into his bunk and lay there thinking about Chet Hollis and the accident and the scream of Wahoo's horse as it went down. His mother told him later that she had come in to say good-bye, but he did not remember her waking him.

5

Two Proposals of Marriage

New saddle or no, Daniel no longer rode out on roundup. Instead he worked the branding pens day after day. He ran errands and oiled harness and sharpened shovels. He split wood for all the stoves on the ranch—maybe all the stoves in the whole world.

He saw the Gladsinger once or twice. He knew he should act friendlier, but the enigmatic young man struck a sour chord somehow. Perhaps it was the tutoring. Right after the problem of the necklace Mr. McGeehan had assigned the Gladsinger the task of tutoring Bridgid. After all, he explained, it was so far for Mom to come. That rankled Daniel. Mom did a good job, and she needed the money more than this Gladsinger did.

As Wahoo felt better he started getting restless. Mr. McGeehan fixed him a deep, comfortable chair on the porch, deciding he would move less sitting up. Daniel realized quickly that reading was not a specialty Wahoo was born to. It took the boy much time and effort to work through relatively short passages. But work he did, studying Daniel's Bible page by page for hours on end.

A week passed, then another. Daniel missed going home because he had to help with Wahoo. Mr. Cadder showed up again, talked to Mr. McGeehan for half an hour, then left. Now a pair of gold cuff links was missing.

The cook got sick (tasted his own cooking, Wick said), and Inez had to cook not just for the main house but for everyone. Contrary was assigned to help her full time. Daniel liked that—he no longer had to haul firewood for her.

The Gladsinger came and went frequently, riding out early in the afternoon and returning late at night. Mr. McGeehan rode out somewhere nearly every Sunday. Daniel saw Bridgid twice in all that time, and on neither occasion was he close enough to say hello. Ranch life was as boring as farm life.

Saturday afternoon Daniel delivered the dirty lunch dishes to the kitchen. Wahoo beckoned him from the porch. He plopped down on the porch rail beside his friend, happy for the chance to sit.

"Dan, this being laid up has its good points."

"Coulda fooled me."

"Oh, it's a nuisance, sure. But look. I got

clear through the New Testament. You know, I heard a lot of that stuff here and there, but I never knew it was in the Bible. And that's not all. I been watching the house and the folks going in and out."

"I'm glad the reading is going well, but what's so great about spying on people?"

"Not spying. Just watching." Wahoo motioned Daniel in closer. "There's a thief around. There has to be. Too many little things—valuable things—are turning up missing."

"Well, it can't be Carrie. She hasn't been here in almost two months."

"Mr. Cadder says it could. The missing stuff could have been taken weeks ago, and someone just now noticed that it's gone. But I don't think so. It could be the Gladsinger. But it might be Inez, too."

"Oh, come on, Wahoo! Why would she want to steal things?"

"The window was open, and I heard her talking to Mr. McGeehan a couple days ago. She feels like she's not getting paid enough. And now with all this extra work and cooking, she's *really* fit to be tied."

Daniel studied a knot in the porch rail, then shook his head. "I just can't see that it's her. She's worked here for years."

"And precious little to show for it, right? Dan, you're never gonna be a detective. Every time I come up with a suspect, you're sure it

49

can't be so. Well, somebody is."

"Yeah. Somebody." Daniel slid off the rail. "Better get back to work. Can I bring you anything?"

"I'm fine." Wahoo pointed out across the yard. "Hey, look. There goes the Gladsinger again. Where does he keep riding off to like that?"

Daniel shrugged. Frankly, he did not care where the fellow went. The Gladsinger's natty black coat disappeared beyond the gate. Out across the yard, draped across corral rails, were those two saddles. Mr. Frazier had told Wick to put new cinches on them. The job was not done yet. He might as well do it. Daniel walked out across the yard.

He knew Mr. Frazier had purchased half a dozen horsehair cinches. They must be somewhere. Maybe in the tack shed? Daniel opened the shed door with a yank; the rusty hinges tended to stick. Something bigger than a mouse made scurrying noises inside, but by the time Daniel's eyes adjusted to the gloom, the creature had hidden itself.

There lay the cinches beside a handful of shiny brass wood screws on the workbench. Daniel picked up the top two and carried them back to the saddles. It was much easier to carry two horsehair cinches to the corral than to muscle those massive saddles around.

The job was done in ten minutes when Wick came walking by. He stopped by the saddles as

Daniel tucked the last latigo end in place. "Why you doing that?"

Daniel stepped back. "Something that had to get done and I could do it."

"I woulda got to it; you don't have to stick your little nose in everything." Wick walked off.

Daniel stood there a while, mad at himself. He should have said something. He could have quoted the apostle Paul: "Whatever ye do do as to the Lord Jesus Christ;" He could have said all sorts of things. He sighed. Wick already thought he was just a silly little kid. Why add to it?

Quitting time arrived eventually. Daniel received his pay, saddled Roller, and rode home faster than usual—this was the first Saturday all month he was going home, and he could not wait to get there. As he rode into his good old farmyard he found out where the Gladsinger had ridden off to on those mysterious excursions. His big-footed sorrel stood tied at the rail by the back door.

Why, by convention, must Sunday dinner always be roasted? No matter. Daniel liked roast beef and roast chicken equally well. He closed the kitchen door behind him and wandered out across the empty yard. The little ones were off somewhere in the noisy distance. Mom, Mr. Carson, and Matt dawdled over after-dinner tea

51

inside, enjoying the Sunday hiatus. Daniel felt restless. For no reason he could perceive he felt out of place in his own home.

"Dan! Wait up!" Carrie came through the kitchen door drying her hands on her apron. They wandered together out across the yard, all springy with tiny green plants, out across the broad flat to the riverside. A red-winged blackbird perched sideways on a tule stalk and creaked at them. Some kind of insects buzzed, hidden.

Daniel tried to think of a conversation topic—any topic. "Uh, Grace says you and Mom went to town yesterday, just the two of you, so you could talk."

"Mm hm."

"What did you talk about?" He did not really care, but it was conversation.

"Oh, woman-to-woman talk. That's why we went alone, without Grace. She was some upset, being left behind."

"I bet. Woman-to-woman. What does that mean?"

"Oh, you know." Carrie shrugged. "We talked about, uh, men and women."

"Who?"

"What?" She frowned, confused.

"Which men and women?"

"Men and women. You know. About *that*."

"Oh." Daniel did not know. He had not the slightest idea, but he decided to pursue the topic no further. Gossip was one of the sins of

52

the flesh in Galatians, so it would be best if he did not know which men and women they had been discussing.

A swooping flock of swallows sailed out across the water in front of them. Daniel admired their untrammeled freedom. "Bank swallows. Must have their nests around here somewhere."

Carrie nodded absently. "Upstream a couple hundred yards. Cliff and I found them last week."

"Mm." His own stretch of river, and Daniel did not know where things were. He was an alien on his own land.

Carrie sat down on the warm soil and tucked her skirts around her ankles. "Bet Bridgid never found her necklace."

"Not that I heard of." Daniel flopped down beside her. He amused himself by flipping leaves and stones into the water.

Carrie talked quietly. "I have a theory about that necklace. The spoon too."

"You and Wahoo. You two should write mystery books."

"Mr. McGeehan took them."

Daniel stared at her. "Oh, that's ridiculous! Why should he?"

"For the excuse to come over here and get to know your mom better. He wouldn't be losing anything, really—the things are his anyway. Later they can just sort of turn up or something. He's been by three or four times since.

Says he admires your mother. Says she has spunk."

"If *spunk* means a mind of your own, she has that and then some." He recalled the smile she gave Mr. McGeehan after she had attended Wahoo's strained back and wrenched knee. It was the same smile she gave to Mr. Carson frequently and, once upon a time, to Pop. A sudden weird thought struck him. "You mean he's courting?!"

"He's not riding clear over here for the cactus pie."

"Well, she's not interested. That I can tell you." He pegged another stone into the river and watched the rings bend with the current. "What was that Gladsinger doing here yesterday, anyway?"

"You mean Galen?"

"Yeah."

Her face turned away slightly. "He's courting, too."

"But Mom's old enough to be his mother! Well, almost."

She glared at him. "I strongly suggest you don't tell your mother that. Of course he's not courting her."

"Well, what other woman would he be interested in? Grace falls in love about every week, but she's just a little girl. Only other female is—" Daniel gasped. "You mean he's sweet on *you*?!"

"He asked me to marry him." She stared out across the water.

"That's the silliest thing I ever heard! And I've listened to Royal's fairy tales."

"What's so silly about it? It's an honor, being asked in marriage."

"But, Carrie! He's so old! He has to be pushing twenty; and you're my age."

"Daniel," she said patiently, "we are not children anymore."

"Then how come I like fishing as much as I ever did?"

"Same reason my father does, probably. It beats working."

Daniel sat and slammed stones into the water, infuriated. She always had some smart answer ready. And she seemed to fit so comfortably into that we-are-grown-up image. And he did not fit anywhere.

"What are you gonna do about it?"

"About what?" Carrie asked.

"Marrying the Gladsinger."

"I haven't decided. Pa says I'm too young. But like your mother says, Galen is a wonderful choice—a man in the faith, dedicated, intelligent, good worker, capable. Hard to find young men like that."

Daniel snorted. He did not say so, but let this Gladsinger tangle with a *real* man—Chet Hollis, for instance—and he would not look so capable. Daniel thought again about Chet back in Texas.

Carrie scooted around to face him squarely. "You're jealous."

"I am not. Why should I want to marry my best friend?"

She laid her hand on his arm—she had to stretch to do it. "We really are best friends, aren't we?"

"I just said so."

"Dan, I don't want that to change. No matter what. No matter what you do or no matter what I do." Her eyes looked frightened, anxious. Why should she be afraid?

"Like getting married?"

"Yes."

"Or stealing things?"

The anxious look blazed instantly into anger. "What a *superb* best friend you are! Maybe Mr. Cadder thinks I'm guilty, but I never thought you'd turn against me!" She was hopping to her feet.

"Hey, look!" Daniel jumped up. "I never said that. I just said—Carrie!"

She was running back toward the house.

How could he have said such a thing? Even if Carrie were guilty, he would stand beside her. He would stick up for her. Like he was sticking up for Jesus lately? He sat down again, glum. He no longer felt like throwing stones into the river.

Behind him Grace's voice called, "Dan, Mom wants you!"

Now what had he done? He could not believe Carrie would say something to get him in trouble. He trudged back to the house and through the kitchen doorway. Matt, Mom, Grace, and Mr. Carson sat at the table. Carrie did too, thoughtfully considering the door lintel as if Daniel were not there.

Mom smiled. "Sit down. Hank and I have been discussing the situation the Lord has put us all in, and we'd like your opinion."

Daniel perked up. People did not normally ask his opinion.

Mr. Carson cleared his throat. "In many ways our two families function as one. We share income, food; the women cook together. Your wages help Carsons as well as Tremains. Since we're so closely knit already, your mother and I feel it would be best if we married and made it a true family."

Carrie squealed for joy.

Grace wrinkled her nose. "Then you'd be our father?"

Mr. Carson shook his head. "Of course not. I could never replace Ira. I wouldn't try. He was one of a kind. The marriage would be a convenience as much as anything—a way to bring the families together honorably."

"And," Mom added, "it eliminates the problem of temptation."

"What temptation?" Daniel asked.

"The—ah—well, Dan, when a man and woman work together closely and know each other as well as Hank and I do, there's bound to be some temptation to sin."

Daniel dropped the subject. "Mourning.

What about mourning? I thought you were supposed to wear black dresses for a year after your husband dies. And a veil."

"That's a nice custom for people back East who don't have ten mouths to feed while they build a farm up from nothing."

Daniel tried to make all this fit in his head. He could not. "And what about Mr. McGeehan? Carrie says he comes around."

Mom glanced at Mr. Carson. She sifted words carefully. "He's a very nice man and prosperous. But his temper and mine wouldn't mix too well. And besides, he has no small children to raise. Hank and I both do."

"So what do you want from us? You seem to have it all figured out."

"Your consent," said Mom. "You see, if you or Grace or Carrie got so upset by this that you ran away, we'd be destroying the families, not saving them."

"Oh, you have my consent! And blessing and everything!" Carrie was so happy she bobbed up and down in her chair. "I think it's just wonderful. So romantic! You two are both so—so—it's just wonderful!"

"Yeah." Daniel mumbled. "Wonderful." He could not wait to ride back to the ranch.

6

A Thief Is Caught

The waning moon, bulgy and pallid, hung on the western edge of the sky as the eastern edge turned from blue-gray to white. Daniel liked dawn, but not nearly as much as sundown. For one thing, sundowns were warmer. He pulled his coat up closer around his neck and unwrapped Roller's reins from the bunkhouse hitch rail. He walked out across the McGeehan ranch yard, Roller plodding complacently along behind. Daniel would saddle his horse, deliver a message out to Mr. Frazier on the north side, then spend the rest of the day splitting rails.

Daniel stopped so suddenly that Roller shouldered into him. Was that a woman's shout? Smoke from the kitchen stove curled into the brightening sky; the only lights in the main house were in the kitchen. Perhaps Inez dropped something. There was the noise again—a woman's cry.

Inez came running out the side door, her white apron tangling about her legs. "*Lad-*

59

rón!" she was screaming. She pointed behind the house and flailed her arms wildly.

Ladrón? What was a *ladrón?* A horse squealed beyond the house. Hoofbeats clattered.

Inez finally remembered the English equivalent. "Thief! Stop, thief!"

The horseman, presumably the thief, appeared beyond the house and rode out the north gate full tilt, low in the saddle. Daniel did not stop to think. He swung up onto Roller's bare back and kicked the startled little horse's corrugated sides. As he reached the gate he glanced back. The Gladsinger was just now running out of the bunkhouse.

Roller, particularly this early in the day, loved to run, sometimes even to crowhop. The little horse was caught up instantly in the spirit of the chase. He leaped a gully and clawed up a cutbank without slowing.

Far ahead on a low hillside a plume of dawn-white dust rose. Daniel began to have misgivings about this pursuit. What would he do if he caught up with the fellow? And the dust cloud, much smaller now because the ground was stony, seemed closer. The thief's horse, at this distance, looked much like Contrary's. In fact the thief himself resembled Contrary.

As they climbed the bajada behind the McGeehan ranch, the terrain got rougher. Daniel very nearly decided to quit. He was going to break Roller's neck and his own as well on this wild ride. He thought fleetingly of the scream of Wahoo's horse in rocks like these. Far behind them, a low cloud of dust picked up the first beams of the rising sun. Daniel would have help—eventually.

It *was* Contrary up ahead. Daniel recognized him clearly now. He would never gain the respect of Wick and the others if he identified Contrary as the thief. He had better stop right now. He would tell whoever was coming up behind him that the robber had escaped.

No! Daniel's loyalty was not to Wick and his pals but to the man who hired him. A sudden, glorious revelation flooded him. Catching Contrary red-handed like this proved Carrie's innocence!

Contrary either dropped or tossed down a wooden box. It flew open, scattering papers and money across the stony hillside. The rider glanced behind him. "Dan! It's only you." He started to rein his horse in.

Daniel kept Roller running. With no rope—not even a saddle—he had no way of keeping Contrary in one place until help arrived. His only weapon was Roller. He decided to use him.

Slowing up should put Contrary's horse off balance. Daniel dragged Roller sideways as they came abreast Contrary. Roller grunted and squealed and plowed into horse and rider with his bony shoulder.

Roller staggered and nearly fell. Daniel dragged him to a stop and wheeled him around. Contrary's horse, belly up on the stones, writhed and wriggled and lurched to its feet. It trotted away toward the ranch, wild-eyed.

Contrary sat still a moment, looking numb. He scrabbled to his feet. "You crazy little kid! You realize what you did to me?" He turned to run.

Daniel thumped his heels into Roller's ribs. The horse lunged forward and bowled Contrary over again. Daniel could hear another horse coming. Was it help, or was it Wick coming to rescue Contrary? He simply could not keep knocking the fellow over forever.

Contrary staggered to his feet, rubbing one knee. The Gladsinger's black hat appeared above the bushes. Never was Daniel so glad to see someone, even the Gladsinger! In fact, as the able young man rode up Daniel cheerfully dumped the whole problem in his lap.

The Gladsinger drew in his horse beside Contrary. His voice was strong, his expression immensely pleased. "Fine work, Dan! A fine job!" Daniel forgot all the less-than-complimentary things he had ever thought about Galen Sanger.

Daniel grinned. "I knew it couldn't be Carrie."

"So did I. And thanks to you, now the world will know. I can take Mr. Contreres here back to the ranch. Will you pick up all those papers that blew away back there?"

"Sure thing!" Daniel watched a moment as Contrary dejectedly found his feet and walked off down the hill. He turned Roller back the way they had come. Here was the box, one hinge broken away. And here were windblown papers all over. The money—five, ten, and twenty-dollar bills—was much the color of the Arizona hillside. Daniel spent twice the time he should have searching, lest one of Mr. McGeehan's bills be overlooked. Joyful, he tucked the wooden box under his arm and rode back to the ranch. He could not wait to see Carrie's face when he told her how he had proved her innocence!

What might a hero's welcome be like? Daniel felt like a hero. After all, he had stopped Contrary single-handed. He had captured a culprit years older and pounds heavier than himself.

No one greeted him as he rode up to the house. Wahoo sat in his chair on the porch. "They're in there, Dan. In Mr. McGeehan's office."

Daniel grinned as he slid off Roller. "Wahoo, I feel so good I could fly! Doing something like that is so—so—I guess Carrie's right. We aren't kids any more."

"Doing what?" Wahoo frowned.

"Catching Contrary. Stopping the thief."

"Who did?"

Daniel was frowning now, too. "I did."

Wahoo's face clouded. "That's not what the Gladsinger's saying. He claims he caught Contrary, and you came along afterward to clean up the loot."

Daniel's heart went thump. "Which one of us do you believe?"

"You. If you said you did, you did. I know that. But I don't think Mr. McGeehan'll take your word, not as glib as that Gladsinger talks."

"But, Wahoo! It was *me* who—" Daniel quit talking. Wahoo was right. "What does Contrary say?"

"Nothing. He won't say nothing."

Daniel sagged against a porch post. The box felt much heavier now than it did a moment ago. "I should've guessed. He acted so take-over. Just stepped right in. He's lying, Wahoo."

Wahoo stared past Daniel, a common habit of his. "Dan, do me one."

"What's that?"

"Ask Mr. McGeehan; work it somehow. I want to talk to Contrary privately; just you and me and him."

Daniel launched himself erect. "I'll try. Gotta take this in anyway. He catches the crook, and I mop up the hillside. Sure." He scuffled in the front door.

The formal parlor felt gloomy despite the morning sun that made the east window glow. Daniel walked on through and rapped on Mr.

McGeehan's office door. The Irishman's voice bellowed a welcome. Daniel stepped inside.

"Ah! Here's me box!" Mr. McGeehan swooped it out of Daniel's hands and plunked it on his desk. He opened it and riffled through the jumbled bills and papers. "Mother McCree, tis all here! Every bit. Splendid, Dan! Splendid!" He picked out one of the bills, a five. "Here, me lad; for being so meticulous in the gathering of it all. Galen says 'twas scattered all topsal teery out there."

Daniel almost reached for the money—half a week's pay—and put both hands behind his back. "I appreciate your thoughtfulness, sir. But I don't expect a reward. I'd like a favor, though."

"Aye?" Mr. McGeehan's eyes narrowed.

"Wahoo and I would like to talk to Contrary out on the porch—just the three of us."

Contrary glanced nervously at Daniel. He did not seem half so nervous about the idea, however, as did the Gladsinger.

"Simple enough request, lad. Aye, why not? Manuel, ye know better than to try to run." Mr. McGeehan handed a heavy pistol to Daniel. "Give this to Wahoo, just to ensure our miscreant's cooperation, aye? I'll be out meself in a few minutes. Must put some things in order before I take him in to the constable."

Daniel followed Contrary out the door, feeling horribly weighted down by the enormous gun. He passed it clumsily to Wahoo. The boy cradled it in his lap, handling it as comfortably as if it were a dessert spoon.

Scowling, Contrary sat on the porch step and studied the dirt at his feet.

Wahoo leaned forward a bit and kept his voice low. "Got some instructions, Con. You let out one little peep about who *really* caught you—especially to Wick and them—and I'll come after you myself. Understand me?"

Contrary shot a quick glance his way and resumed interest in the dirt.

Daniel was too surprised to speak. Why did Wahoo say that?

Wahoo continued, "And now I want to know if you're the one who took all those other things. Just you and me and Dan here, and we promise never to tell a soul. Not a word. Was it you?"

Contrary looked up at Daniel, so Daniel met his eye, trying to look friendly. Contrary turned to Wahoo. "No. I didn't take nothing else."

"But you know who did."

"No."

"If you didn't take anything else, Con, why'd you swipe the box?" Wahoo's voice did not accuse. It sounded caring and soft. Daniel felt certain Wahoo really did care.

Apparently so did Contrary. "I was only gonna take that one thing. I knew there was money in it. Then when the other guy got caught—the thief, you know?—everyone would think he took the box too."

66

"Didn't it ever occur to you that you might get caught?"

Contrary shrugged. "Sure, sorta. But I'm in the house, and my horse is waiting out back; and no one else was around, I thought. There it was, lying open, just setting right there. Begging me. 'Yoo hoo, Contreres, here I am,' it says. 'Nobody gonna know.' The temptation was too big to resist."

Wahoo sat back in his chair. This time he stared through Contrary.

Mr. McGeehan clapped his hat on as he came out the door. He retrieved his gun from Wahoo. "Come along, Manuel. Dan, 'tis wise never to accept charity, but this be an earned reward." He pressed a coin into Daniel's hand and strode out across the yard with Contrary.

Daniel opened his hand. "A five-dollar gold piece."

"It's the least he could do. Take it." Wahoo shifted in his chair with a little grimace. "I have some ideas about this case."

"Case?"

"Yeah. I been thinking. What future do you have being a cowboy? So you work your way up to foreman. Or maybe you never do. Peterson, he's as good as Mr. Frazier, but he's never gonna be a foreman. His whole life he'll be a forty-a-month cowboy. I think maybe I'll be a detective instead."

"Aw, come on, Wahoo. You're the best cowboy in the world. A rope, a gun, a horse—all of it."

67

"Sure. Detectives have to be good with a gun. And I don't doubt a rope would be handy. And how do you get anywhere except on a horse? You see? Working cattle is good training for being a detective."

"So who'll hire you? Mr. McGeehan? Mr. Cadder?"

"There's agencies, Dan. Pinkerton's a big one. They hire the detectives. Then people who need a detective—the clients—they hire the agency. It's big money. And lots more exciting than driving cows."

"And this is your first big case."

"Yep." Wahoo grinned. "Think I have it figured out too, only I need a little more time. Gotta get on my feet."

Daniel thought about those things a moment. A detective? It would be more fun than farming, but surely not more fun than the life of a cowboy. Cowboys stick together. And Daniel thought of Contrary. Was he a friend at all to Contrary? Hardly.

"Wahoo, suppose there's anything we can do to help Contrary?"

"I don't know. What a fool stunt, trying to steal that box. Contrary ain't no thief, Dan. Leave your week's pay out on your bunk and it's still there when you reach for it. Wick, Mr. Frazier, me—none of us would steal. I can't understand why Contrary did."

"There was lots more money in the box than just a week's pay, or a month's." Daniel

68

stepped off the porch. "I still gotta deliver that message to Mr. Frazier. Anything I can get you?"

Wahoo shook his head. Daniel could tell that his thoughts were on things far away. Daniel walked out across the yard leading Roller.

His own mind was jumbled. How could the Gladsinger take credit for Daniel's derring-do? And why should Wahoo abet it?

He thought of Contrary's temptation and why he succumbed. Apparently the size of the temptation has much to do with it.

Daniel suddenly hatched an idea, and what a marvelous idea! He would use his gold piece as bait. He would set it out somewhere and keep an eye on it from afar. Whoever took it—that was the thief! He would set a trap, catch the thief, and solve this mystery once for all. Wahoo might be a detective, but Daniel would be a trapper.

With a broad, happy grin he flapped the saddle blanket across Roller's back and reached for his saddle.

7

Wick's Invitation

Where should he set his bait? Daniel tucked his quilt under his mattress and climbed down off the bunk. How about that table by the door? He laid the gold piece on the table and studied the effect. Pretty good. Maybe the wood stove, now that the fire was out? No. If the thief thought he might burn his fingers, he would not touch it.

Wait! How could he prove, once the thief had grabbed it, that this particular coin was his? Daniel fished out his pocket knife and cut two tiny matching notches in the coin's edge. That made it one of a kind. He contemplated the window sill (too obvious) and the little table by Wahoo's bed. Finally he left the coin in the place he had first considered, the table by the door, and walked out into the bright morning light.

Now he must find a good place from which to watch. He must see exactly who entered and left the bunkhouse without looking suspicious himself. He stationed himself against the water trough on the far side of the yard. No good. Whoever saw him here looking idle would put him to work elsewhere. He must busy himself. But how?

The shed door swung open, and the Gladsinger came out. He carried a toolbox and some parts and pieces Daniel did not recognize. He came whistling over to the water trough and dropped the toolbox near Daniel's feet.

"Good morning, Dan. You're assigned to windmill duty, too?"

"What?"

"The windmill broke down last night. I'm supposed to fix it. I thought perhaps you were told to help."

"Oh." Here was the perfect thing! Daniel could watch the bunkhouse constantly. "No, but I'd sure love to help you out."

The Gladsinger smiled and nodded. He grew serious. "Dan, I must apologize right now for that business about Manuel Contreres yesterday—taking the credit, as it were. You see, Mr. McGeehan was about ready to dismiss me. Spring round-up is about finished. His books are in order again. He's considering asking your mother to come back as tutor. I was desperate, and there was a chance to ingratiate myself to him. I've been looking ever since then for the opportunity to tell you I'm sorry. It was wrong."

What could he say? Daniel knew Mr.

McGeehan let go all but a few old hands (Mr. Frazier, Peterson, and them) as soon as the spring rush of work was finished. He had not thought that the Gladsinger might need the opportunity Manuel Contreres presented. Daniel certainly did not. He would be let go in a few weeks anyway. He mumbled something about the apology being accepted.

The Gladsinger smiled warmly. "I thought Carrie was overstating your Christian virtues. She was not. Thank you, Dan." He rubbed his hands together. "Well, the windmill. I suspect the eccentric is broken. We'll climb up there and dismantle it as a first step."

"Climb clear up there?"

"You aren't afraid, are you?"

"No." Daniel was not afraid. But how could he run to the bunkhouse and nab the thief—spring his trap—if he was stuck on top of the windmill with both hands full of incomprehensible parts?

"Good morning, Galen." Her voice made Daniel jump. In his surveillance of the bunkhouse he had not noticed the yard or main house. How could he have missed this lovely vision? Bridgid glided up to them. Her copper hair glinted, and she looked gorgeous in that yellow-green dress.

"Good morning, Bridgid." The Gladsinger smiled at her briefly and returned to digging in his toolbox.

Daniel mumbled something, although he

had not been included in her original greeting.

The Gladsinger shaded his eyes and looked at the creaking vanes far above them. "I think we're going to need the big pipe wrench for this, Dan. Be back in a moment." He nodded mechanically toward Bridgid and walked off to the shed.

Normally Daniel would be ecstatic over this chance to talk to Bridgid alone. But she stared past him, iceberg-cold, and said nothing.

Mom was always telling Daniel to take the bull by the horns, and it always worked for her. "You act mad about something. What's wrong?"

"Oh, nothing," she said airily. Her voice hardened. "That is, if one does not mind consorting with thieves."

"You still think Carrie took that necklace?"

"Maybe aye, maybe nay."

"What does that mean?"

Bridgid looked him right in the eye. "You had just as much opportunity as she, evensay more. You and perhaps your mother as well."

"Hey, now just a minute! You want to sling mud at me, that's one thing. But not my mother, and not Carrie, either!"

She stamped her pretty foot. "You'd lie through your teeth to protect Carrie! Both of you. And Galen goes riding clear over there every spare minute he gets. What's the matter with you stupid people? She's as plain as a washtub and twice as rough! She has skin like a gold panner. She's a peasant! A—a—oh, you two are both disgusting!" She whipped around, her skirts rustling, and marched off to the house.

Daniel sighed very heavily and leaned against the weathered windmill braces. The Gladsinger came out, whistling as cheerily as if the world had not turned gray. Daniel remembered to glance toward the bunkhouse. Deserted.

At the main house Wahoo sat on the porch as usual, poring over the Bible. Bridgid paused at the steps and curtsied. Daniel could not hear, but she must have spoken to Wahoo. He looked up, nodded, and went back to reading. After a long pause she glanced back toward Daniel and went inside.

"*I said,* 'You climb up that side, and I'll go up this side.' " The Gladsinger jarred him out of his thoughts.

"Sure." Much as he hated the thought, Bridgid's jealousy made her a suspect, too, her motive vengeance rather than greed. Daniel barked his shin on a cross-brace, tore the skin off his knuckle trying to loosen a rusted bolt, and got three splinters. The whole morning went that way.

At lunch Daniel made certain he was first into the bunkhouse. He pocketed the gold piece and set it out again before he left. It was there when he returned for supper. Perhaps he was being too impatient. It might take days for the thief to be in the right place at the right time.

Wednesday evening the gold piece was still untouched—the bait not taken. Daniel climbed to his bunk and flopped down, waiting for supper. Tomorrow he would mention his plan to Wahoo. Perhaps Wahoo would have some ideas about getting faster results.

Wick's bunk went *whump* as he threw himself on it. "We gotta think of some way to get that Gladsinger."

The young, buck-toothed cowboy called Beaver tossed his hat on his bunk and sprawled out in the chair by the stove. "Don't let Mr. Frazier hear that, or he'll fire the lot of us. He's mad enough to do it anyway."

Wick snorted. "I get paid by the week, not by the cow. Don't matter to me how many cows I pop outta the brush."

"Yeah," said Beaver. "Listen to me anyway. No talk about revenge where anyone can hear you."

The short, dumpy cowboy called O'Toot nodded. " 'Sides, it was partly Contrary's fault. Stupid is what it was."

"Stupid. Right!" Wick said. "One little stupid mistake, and the Gladsinger acts like the Supreme Court. Well, that was *his* stupid mistake, picking on Contrary. He'll pay for it, too."

Daniel realized now why Wahoo had insisted

that the Gladsinger get the credit. Wahoo was wise, all right.

A wooden match scritched and hissed near Wick's bunk. A curl of cigar smoke wandered toward the ceiling. "Y'know," said Wick, "Wahoo's the one I got my eye on. The way he stares at you like that."

"Yeah." Beaver poured himself some coffee. "He's spooky, all right. Don't never joke or laugh. Keeps to hisself. And he can shoot the feelers off a cockroach."

Daniel was going to speak up, but he was afraid to. Wahoo was perfectly warm and friendly, once you knew him.

"Tell you what's even more suspicious." Wick's voice paused. A smoke ring floated by. "We know Wahoo maybe two years off and on, right? When in them two years did he ever read anything?"

"Not except now," said O'Toot. "Reading that Bible now."

"Right. Who knows if he can read atall? But he's got that Bible in his lap all day. Now why should he be doing that except to look all pious and holy?"

"Hey!" Beaver nearly dropped his coffee mug. "Then maybe he's the one, and he's not really laid up at all. Maybe that strained back business is all a sham."

"Wahoo picks up an expensive little trinket now and then, and Contrary picks up the jail sentence. Whaddaya think, Handy?"

Handy's real name was Manolo. But his nickname was Mano and *mano* in Spanish means "hand." He leaned on a bunk support. "Soun's good to me. I don' never like that Wahoo ennyhow."

"Dan does, don't you, Dan?" Wick called. "Like Wahoo?"

Daniel's breastbone tickled, partly because he was being drawn into this hideous speculation and partly because he feared for Wahoo's reputation. He twisted around on his stomach to perch with both elbows on the edge of his bunk. "Yeah, I like Wahoo. And I believe him when he says his back's hurt."

Wick waved a finger at Daniel. "You gotta learn, boy, never to believe anything anyone says. Not anything. Where'd he get that Bible, anyway?"

The apostle Paul said to defend the Word in season and out of season, and this seemed as out of season as you could get. Daniel felt so nervous his voice shook a little. "Well, Wick. See, last fall Wahoo developed this interest in Jesus, and—uh—I loaned him my Bible so he could read up on it. Being he can only sit."

"*Your* Bible!" Beaver drained his coffee. "You don't look like no preacher."

"That's right; I remember." Wick waved his stinky cigar. "Mr. Frazier says Dan here and his pa were spouting the Bible the first time he ever met 'm. Forgot about that."

Handy grinned. "Better talk to us down here,

78

Dan, while you got de chance. You be de only cowboy in heaven, 'cause we're having too much fun to go, eh?"

Everyone laughed but Daniel. His ears burned. Did they not know they were insulting God? Of course they did not. And Daniel was too shy, too scared to tell them so. He felt disgusted with himself, truly disgusted.

Wick swung his legs off his bunk and sat up. "Why, I bet you're one of them poor little kids who grew up religious." The tone of his voice mocked the words. "Bet you don't know the first thing about real living."

"Oh, I don't know—" Daniel tried to look nonchalant.

"Which is higher—a straight or a flush?"

"Huh?"

"What do you call a jack in euchre?" Wick was gloating now. "How much is a red chip worth? Say, how good do you do in a fight anyway?"

"Never got in a real good fight. Don't know whether—"

They were laughing again. In a way Daniel felt better that they were laughing at him and not at God.

Daniel brightened. "But I got this good friend in Texas named Chet Hollis, and nobody's better at fighting than he is."

"Oh, sure!" Beaver cackled. "My little brother had this imaginary friend too. You can't *believe* all the things that transparent kid could do."

79

"He's not transparent, and he's not imaginary. And he's bigger'n you are."

Wick stood up, almost nose to nose with Daniel. "Y'know, Beave, we oughta take this little boy to town with us Saturday."

"You crazy? Little kid like that can ruin the whole night!"

"Teach him what living's all about. Show him the part of town he ain't been in." Wick gave Daniel a friendly slap on the arm that bowled him sideways. "Right, Dan?"

The dinner gong rang. Daniel was forgotten as the boys poured out of the bunkhouse. What did Wick mean by that? "Teach you about living"? It sounded ominous, unwholesome. On the other hand, it might well give Daniel the chance to discuss Jesus in a more conducive atmosphere. In a way he looked forward very much to next Saturday night.

8

The Bait Is Taken

"Forget it. No." Wahoo hobbled along on homemade crutches, working his way from the bunkhouse to the summer kitchen. Daniel walked alongside, dragging his feet through the powdery dust.

Wahoo paused to readjust his weight. "Wick and those lop-ears don't have a brain between them. Their idea of a good time is getting drunk and losing a poker game. Go home Saturday night like you always do, and forget about Wick and Beave and them."

"Wahoo, I'm not just a little kid any more."

"That's what worries me. You're old enough to get in trouble and too young to know you're doing it. I was your age once; I know. Problem was, I didn't have a good, upstanding mother like you got."

Upstanding. Upstanding, perhaps, but frustrating. Mom and Mr. Carson were serious about this marriage business—serious enough to set a date in less than two weeks. Daniel could not understand Carrie's enthusiasm for the whole idea.

Wahoo was teetering along a little faster now. "You're gonna get enough temptations in this life without going out looking for 'm. The boozing, the card playing—all that stuff— starts out looking harmless and then sorta just sucks you in deeper and deeper. Ain't no sense following a fellow who's going in the wrong direction. Tell Wick you ain't interested."

"Then I could never reach them at all. I couldn't talk to them or anything. It's all right, Wahoo. I know what I'm doing."

Wahoo snorted derisively.

Daniel decided to change the subject. "What are you doing this morning?"

"Peeling potatoes. You?"

"Fixing that door on the root cellar. Gives me a good chance to keep an eye on the bunk-house."

Wahoo stopped by the door of the summer kitchen. "Why?"

"I got a trap set. A five-dollar gold piece by the door. Nobody took it yet, though. Any suggestions?"

"Yeah." Wahoo grimaced and adjusted his weight again, carefully. "The stuff was stolen here, not the bunkhouse. Set your trap here around the main house."

The light dawned. "Of course! The necklace, cuff links—all stolen here. But that means someone in the house is responsible."

"Maybe," said Wahoo cryptically. "I got some ideas. Anyway, try your bait here, and keep a close eye on it." He swung the door open and lurched his body and crutches, a clumsy tripod, into the gloom.

Daniel ran back to the bunkhouse and scooped his coin off the table. He considered new locations as he crossed the yard. He put the coin on a windowsill near the door. Although he could not see the window from the root cellar, he could still see who came and went. He walked around to the root cellar to get busy.

"Aaak!" O'Toot jumped a foot. "What are you doing back here?"

Daniel had jumped just as high. He began unloading tools from his belt and pockets. "I'm supposed to take the cellar doors off, straighten 'm, and nail some braces on. Wanna help?"

"Not really." O'Toot sat down, his back leaning on the wall, and drew his legs up. Daniel observed privately that O'Toot's legs were so stubby that he was not much shorter sitting than standing.

The iron screws holding the door hinges had corroded. The slots had rusted nearly full. Daniel gouged at the slots with the corner of the screwdriver, trying to scrape them deeper. He would love to replace them with non-corroding brass screws, but he had noticed in getting the tools that all the brass screws were gone.

A rustle off by the ocotillo fence startled him.

He snapped around to look that way as a little brown blob disappeared through a leafy gap in the fence. He glanced at O'Toot. "Ground squirrel?"

"Or a pack rat. Didn't see." O'Toot could be helping with this door. The screws would not back out; the wood would not tear away under the crowbar.

"What are you doing back here, O'Toot?"

"Thinking. Can't just sit and think when I'm with the others. Always someone talking, messing around, joking. I like to just sit and think now and then." One rusty hinge gave way. Three to go.

Daniel shifted his attention to the top of the door. " 'Bout what?"

"Don't know." O'Toot looked at him. "Sounds crazy, don't it. Maybe I am going crazy. I want to think about things, but I don't know what."

"Not so crazy." Aha! One screw pulled loose and another broke off. He had a second hinge free. "You have this empty space inside, and you want to fill it but nothing fits. And you don't know what to try for size next."

"Yeah!" O'Toot's voice sounded a little awed. "That's the very feeling."

Daniel was only half thinking about O'Toot. He had one hinge loose on the second cellar door. He used the screwdriver like a cold chisel. It worked, but the idea did not serve the screwdriver too well. As he dragged the last hinge free he noticed the screwdriver blade looked a little mangled. The left-hand door was crookedest. Daniel stood it on edge and started pounding.

"Dan? You ever find anything that fits?"

"Yeah. Jesus takes care of all that, as much as you let Him. Here. Hold this on edge while I pound, can you?" Daniel tipped the door toward O'Toot. "Jesus takes care of the tough stuff I can't handle on my own."

"For instance?"

"Hard questions, like why bother living? That gets heavy sometimes. Like when my Pop died last winter. No problem, from God's point of view. What to do about difficult situations that come up. But mostly He just fills up that hole inside."

"Wick's right. You really are a Bible pounder."

"Not as much as I oughta. When you guys were talking before supper—remember?—I should have spoken up and didn't. I know it isn't right, but when Wick's around I lose my nerve sorta."

"He's a nice guy, y'know. Down inside."

" 'Spect so." Daniel turned his attention to the other door, the one that sagged less. "Really wish you could meet Chet Hollis, though. He and his pa would sell whiskey around to hotels here and there before they got saved. Talk about enjoying a fight. Chet just loved a scrap."

"They don't do it anymore?"

"Chet knew Jesus wouldn't like it, so when he accepted Jesus he busted up his still. I imagine it was something of a struggle for him. Nothing he liked better than raising a ruckus."

"Why?"

"What?"

"Why'd he change? Who made him?"

Daniel stood up straight. "Nobody *made* him, O'Toot. When you realize how much Jesus gave up for you, it's a lot easier to act the way He wants you to. You see, Jesus is the Son of God—He *is* God. He knows everything and can do anything. But He gave all that up and became a plain old ordinary person. And then He even gave that up and let other plain old people torture Him to death. And that's a whole pile of giving up."

"Never heard it that way before."

"Just telling you why Chet wanted to change his ways. Jesus never did anything wrong, so He had nothing to die for. So He could die for all the wrong things everyone else did, including Chet and me. And you, if you'll accept Him."

"*Me!* Now don't you go preaching at me!"

Daniel laid the two doors out side by side. They looked pretty straight. "You're the one who asked, you know. I was just telling you what I know to be a fact."

"I wasn't asking for no preaching."

"Sure you were, soon as you started talking

86

about a lost or empty feeling. Look, O'Toot, you don't have to buy it. But unless you do, you're never gonna be happy—I mean, really happy. You think it was noisy a minute ago; wait 'til I fetch some boards to nail on as braces. Be right back."

Daniel jogged off to the lumber pile behind the barn. It only now dawned on him exactly what he and O'Toot had been talking about. He allowed himself a private little grin. Yes, he would go with Wick to town on Saturday night. *Just look—you can talk so comfortably under the right circumstances and surroundings.*

He did not expect O'Toot to be there when he got back, but there the boy sat, next to the cellar doors. Daniel dropped the saw and boards on a pile.

"Dan. Lemme ask you this—"

Wahoo came lurching out the kitchen door as Daniel walked by. "Get your cellar doors fixed?"

Daniel paused to wait for him, grinning. "Yeah. And you won't believe who I was talking to. You been peeling potatoes the whole day in there?"

"Inez was putting up strawberry jam, so I helped with that. I scoured a thousand pots she hadn't got to lately, too." He started out across the broad, dusty yard. "She can keep you busy for a lifetime. Hey, I was reading some at lunch time. Corinthians."

"Which Corinthians?"

"First one, I think. Chapter nine. You know how you said if Wick don't respect you, you can't talk to them?"

"Yeah, but—" Daniel was particularly anxious to tell Wahoo all about O'Toot's interest.

"No buts. Paul says that to the Jews he acted like a Jew and to the weak he acted weak. You know that part. Anyway, Dan, Paul started out where the other fellow was, but *he didn't stay there.* Got me?"

"Yeah, but—"

"You start out where Wick is maybe, but you don't stay with him. You bring him around to where you are. And where you are is behaving yourself and not ramming around town doing the stuff they do."

Why argue? Wahoo's mind was set. Well, so was Daniel's. He knew what he was doing. You can look at mud without getting your hands dirty.

The coin! Daniel had forgotten about his bait. "Wait a minute, Wahoo. Gotta get my gold piece." He ran back to the house, to the porch, to the windowsill.

The gold coin was gone.

In its place lay a shiny brass wood screw.

9

Fight!

A heady exhilaration comes from riding in a group. The cumulative clatter and sense of power is greater than that which the same number of riders could ever generate individually. Daniel rode in the midst of this power and clatter surrounded by Wick and his pals. Daniel was loving every minute of this ride into town.

In Tubac the group separated. Wick disappeared into a tavern, and the other three rode off to visit Contrary in the jail. Daniel felt sorely tempted to just ride on home. What if Contrary told them who really caught him?

Daniel's pay jingled in his pocket, but he did not really feel like buying anything. It was an unmentioned rule that everyone's pay went to Mom unspent. She would sit at the table for an hour as her tea grew cold, dividing coins and bills into little piles. This pile went for the month's land payment. This one was the fabric for Grace's new dress (her old one, nearly outgrown, was ready to pass on to Rachel). That large pile would buy groceries, and these tiny ones would pay for the miscellaneous necessities of the month.

The sun disappeared completely beyond its long shadows. Gloomy shade filled the spaces between the quiet little adobe buildings and smothered the narrow side streets. Daniel had never been in town after dark. He did not like it. The streets seemed deserted, ominous.

The only store window with a light in it blinked dark. A small hunchbacked figure appeared in its doorway, rattled a key in a lock, and shuffled off down the street. The only lights left shone in the windows of back street houses and in the town's two little taverns.

Daniel buttoned his coat. It was not so cold, but it felt that way. He rode upstreet to the town pump and slid off Roller. He admired the town pump. It stood brazen in the very middle of the street. No horse or wagon dared hit it, for it was much too solid. The water trough, a stonemason's nightmare, had to be eight feet long. Round river rocks of all sizes protruded from its mortar in haphazard bumps. Ah, but the pump itself was a carpenter's dream. The barrel of the pump was a waterproof wooden box a foot wide and taller than Daniel's head. The spout was half a mesquite limb hollowed out.

Daniel pumped water into the trough for the pure pleasure of using the pump. He stood on its little wooden platform and whanged the heavy oak handle up and down enthusiastically. The pump coughed, wheezed, gurgled, and sent a trickle of cold, clear water out the spout. Ostensibly Daniel was pumping for Roller, but his horse was not thirsty tonight. Eventually he quit and led Roller down the street toward the jail.

Daniel froze as whooping riders burst out onto the street ahead. O'Toot led the pack. He slowed beside Daniel. "Whatcha going that way for, Dan?" O'Toot called and bucketed on by. Wick materialized in front of the saloon across the way and swung aboard his horse. Daniel turned back. He, too, would have mounted up, but his friends were dismounting near the pump. No doubt they were thinking of watering their horses. Daniel tugged on Roller and dragged him up the street to join them.

He stopped short; he could not believe what he saw! That figure crossing the darkening street up ahead was Carrie; Daniel was certain. The size, the firm way she walked, the way she carried her head—Carrie, all right. He hung back, hoping she would not notice him. It was not exactly that he was ashamed of his raucous friends up ahead there, it was simply that—yes, that was it exactly. He was ashamed to be seen with Wick and the others.

"Welly, welly, welly. Look who's here! What are you doing in town so late, Miss Icicle?" Wick's voice, overly loud, sounded strangely mocking.

Daniel wondered that, too. Did that mean Mom or Mr. Carson was in town tonight? Oh, he certainly hoped not! He dropped Roller's reins and hurried forward.

Carrie had stopped, engulfed by McGeehan ranch hands. There was no gentle smile of recognition, that pleasant smile in which she specialized. She looked terrified. Daniel could not make out her words from there, but she was pleading with the boys to leave her alone.

Daniel pushed past Handy's little horse. He had never seen Carrie look so frightened, not even when that white bull entered the Carson yard years ago. She knew these fellows. But then Wick was frightening him, too. The boisterous joking, the demeanor had faded from happy into dangerous somehow.

Carrie's voice cracked a bit. "Mrs. Tremain is right over there on side street finishing up some sewing. She's expecting me back, and she's going to come looking for me. Please, I have to go."

Beaver made some crude sort of remark and Handy another. Apparently everyone considered them funny. All except Daniel laughed uproariously. Daniel would never in a million years dream of saying stuff like that in front of a girl—especially not in front of Carrie who was in addition, his best friend. Wick reached out to tickle her cheek, and she knocked his hand away. More inane laughter.

For once Daniel remembered to ask God for

help *before* he dived into a project instead of afterward. His mental prayer was unusually short, even for him—"Help, please!"—but sufficient. After all, God was adequately apprised of the situation.

Daniel lunged solidly into Wick, shouldering him aside.

"Hey, what—! Oh, it's you. For a short kid, you sure are clumsy, Dan. Watch it."

"That's just the trouble," Daniel grinned. "I'm so short I couldn't see what was happening. Don't mind if I sit up front, do you?"

Everyone, including Wick, laughed, and Beaver gave him a comradely whop on the shoulder.

"Besides," said Daniel, "I must really be missing something. It seems plain stupid to me to tease a girl the way you guys are doing. If you're so grown up, why are you acting like ten-year-olds?"

Wick laughed again. "We promised to show you what living is all about. So sit down in your front seat here and listen up, 'cause you're gonna learn a thing or three."

More outlandish laughter.

Daniel shook his head. "I never was one to just sit around and watch." No one would be expecting him to move quickly. He slammed his elbow sideways into Wick's ribs and pushed him backward. He heard Wick grunt. He swung his left arm wildly, aimlessly into Beaver. He grabbed Carrie's wrist, swung her

93

around, and flung her up against the town pump. He wheeled around and planted himself in front of her. With the pump and trough behind them, they now had only three sides to defend. Four startled mouths dropped open in dumb amazement.

Daniel kept his voice low, pretending he was not afraid. "I mean that you should leave her alone. Go have fun someplace else."

O'Toot wagged his head. "Well, I never."

Wick drew an experimental deep breath and rubbed his ribs. "Just 'cause we're friends and we work together, I'll forget you just about busted my side just now. But you get on that slabsided nag of your'n and go home, little boy. Right now!"

Handy was snickering. "'Sides, little boy, you gotta turn de odder cheek, 'member? Blessed are de peacemakers."

"That's probably what the moneychangers said just before Jesus turned their tables upside down. You guys know what's right and wrong, and you know which side of it you're on. Leave her alone."

O'Toot licked his lips and took a step backwards. If it came to a showdown, would he be ally or enemy?

Beyond them in the gloom of near night a horseman was approaching. His form was neither Mr. Carson's nor Mr. Cadder's. Which side would he take, or would he become involved at all?

Wick moved in closer. His veneer of friendship had disappeared completely. "Nobody stands up to me and says 'That's naughty,' especially not a high-hat little goody like you."

Daniel never did sort out exactly what happened next, because several things happened simultaneously. Wick took a swing at Daniel, and Beaver was moving forward. Carrie started rattling the pump handle. Handy was coming at him, too. Daniel doubled up and rammed forward; his head slammed into Wick's belly. The belt buckle hurt.

A long arm from nowhere knocked Daniel off his feet. As he landed in the dust, Daniel's mind recorded briefly: *Since this is the first fight I tried, it figures I'll lose.* O'Toot loomed above him—so much for an ally in the face of danger. O'Toot yelped and collapsed beneath a heavy *clunk*!

Wahoo swung his crutch up and yelled, "Go get 'm, Dan!"

Handy fell upon Daniel before he could reach his knees, and the two of them grappled in the dirt. Daniel expected Wick to pile on, too, or at least start kicking him. He did not.

A wild "Yah-hoo!", gloriously happy in tone, came from the direction of the mysterious horseman. Handy went, "Ooof!" and rolled aside. Carrie stood over him with that heavy oak pump handle. That was what she had been doing—unbolting the pump handle! Daniel squirmed to his feet.

Beaver and Wahoo were struggling over the crutch. Beaver had Wahoo bent back nearly double against the rocky water trough. Wahoo's back must hurt terribly. Daniel grabbed two handfuls of Beaver's hair and dragged him away. He swung Beaver, still by the hair, toward Carrie. She hit him in the side with her pump handle.

Whoever had yelled, "Yah-hoo," was really cleaning up on Wick. Mr. Cadder came waddling up shouting, "That's all! Stop it!"—but not before the stranger had dumped Wick in the dirt.

Mr. Cadder stood there with his long-barreled pistol aimed at a star. "Hit's over with! That's all! Now what's going on here?"

Carrie dropped her pump handle, ran over, and buried her head in Mr. Cadder's ample chest, sobbing. "Oh, Mr. Cadder! I was so scared! They were—they said—they were—oh, Mr. Cadder!"

The constable tried to look official and pat Carrie's head at the same time. "Here, here, Miss Carson. It's all over. We'll just haul this whole caboodle down to the jailhouse where we got some light. Sort things out there. Hit's all right now."

Handy sat with both legs straight out in front of him, staring blankly at the toes of his boots. Beaver was taking plenty of time to stand up, and Wick had not even started the process yet. O'Toot climbed cautiously to his feet, keeping a suspicious eye on Wahoo.

We are not little children any more, Daniel thought briefly. Carrie certainly looked pretty little right now. But who was the yah-hoo-er, the mysterious horseman? All Daniel could see in the darkness were bulky shoulders, a thick shock of hair, and—

"Chet! I don't believe it! Carrie, it's Chet! It really is!"

Daniel, Chet, and then Carrie hugged and laughed and backslapped and waltzed each other around. And Mr. Cadder, swamped by despondent losers on the one hand and ecstatic winners on the other, could only stand there and look confused.

10

Undone by a Pocket Watch

Mr. McGeehan's buckboard bounced and pitched the worst of any Daniel had ever ridden in. Wahoo was not driving fast either. Daniel stood on the floorboard and hooked both elbows over the back of the wagon seat. That put his head about even with Wahoo's and Chet's—a handy arrangement, for the buckboard was as noisy as it was springy.

"So when Dan took off to town with them yay-hoos," Wahoo was saying, "I got worried. Asked Mr. McGeehan to borry his buckboard here, since I can't ride a horse much yet, and came in to keep an eye on old Dan. Ensure he didn't get in too much trouble, you might say."

Daniel leaned forward. "I heard Pop say once that Arizona here is seven hundred and fifty miles from Springer. When did you leave Texas, Chet? And why'd you come clear out here?"

Chet leaned back to talk to him better. "Remember when Ma and Pa accepted Jesus? And Pa kind of did it against his better judgment? Ma is doing just fine, but Pa's slipping back into his old ways. I was afraid I might let him rub off on me and slip back, too, so I figured it was time to leave home."

A little light dawned in Daniel's mind. "Sort of avoiding temptation, you mean."

"Yeah. Yeah, that's right." Chet nodded. "Figured I could find work here about as easy as anywhere. 'Sides, I missed you. Sure hate to hear about your pa's passing, though. He was a fine man."

"Yeah." But Daniel was thinking about other things, mostly temptation. Mom said that she and Mr. Carson were marrying to avoid temptation. Rather, were they not simply eliminating it? Chet was running from it. Contrary had yielded to it only once. But that one time had messed him up for years to come.

How was Daniel handling this business of temptation? He was being protected from it, that was how—protected by a friend true enough to bounce clear into Tubac with a sore back in this jostling buckboard.

Chet and Wahoo were less interested in the ramifications of temptation than in the fight.

Chet was grinning. "Sure was fun. That's the first time in a long time I tied into a real good set-to. Your Wick isn't too bad as fighting goes."

"Y'know," said Wahoo, "I don't doubt Mr. Frazier will hire you on. With Wick and the boys cooling off in the pokey for three days, and Contrary in there for quite some time, he's down a couple hands. Doubt Wick will give you any trouble around the ranch—not the way you introduced yourself to him tonight."

"I'm sorry about O'Toot mostly." Daniel's voice bounced because the buckboard did. "Now he's never gonna listen to anything I say."

"Not atall, Dan." Wahoo grinned. "You not only got his attention, you got his respect. He'll listen. Bet he'll come around, too."

Daniel liked that idea. Wahoo knew human nature; if Wahoo said it, Daniel did not doubt it. "Chet? Did you know it was me when you waded into that fight?"

"Nope. Your voice has changed and you've growed. I just figured any guy who took on odds like that deserved a helping hand."

Daniel glanced behind them. Roller plodded along, tied at the back, his nose nearly touching the floorboard. Beside him, Chet's Tornado still pranced, slim and black. Chet's little horse had come how many miles, and he still looked fresh.

The moon was high already; it must be very late. That particular moon phase was labeled "gibbous," but Daniel could not remember where he had learned that. He felt very sleepy.

When they reached the ranch Daniel had every intention of looking up Scripture passages about temptation, but he fell asleep too quickly. It was four o'clock the next afternoon before he got around to borrowing his Bible back from Wahoo.

Daniel wished they would hurry. His shoulders ached from holding this heavy window cornice up. He felt wobbly standing precariously on this kitchen chair.

Mom stood up by his feet and stepped back. She tugged a bit at the window drapery and smiled. "What do you think, Mr. McGeehan?"

"Elegant it is, elegant indeed! Y're an artist, Mrs. Tremain."

Daniel was unimpressed. The McGeehan parlor here was dark enough without curtains. Those new draperies, fashionable though they might be, made it even gloomier.

"It's a bit plain," Bridgid sniffed. "but I suppose you can't expect miracles out here in a blazing wilderness." She sat pouting in the farthest, darkest corner.

Daniel knew the reason for her petulance. Carrie was here at the ranch today helping Mom sew Mr. McGeehan's new draperies. Actually, Carrie was not here at this moment. She was outside at the wagon, digging through a box for Mom's long shears. Carrie was becoming almost as fine a seamstress as Mom. Why did Bridgid have to be so critical of her? Daniel would never understand women.

Mom knelt beside the chair and stabbed brass pins into the curtains, marking places to be hemmed. "You can put that down now, Dan. This fabric is as lovely as any I ever saw back in Illinois. Where did you ever find it, Mr. McGeehan?"

"Me sister sent it out from New York, knowing I needed parlor draperies." He sat down and drained his teacup. "I must write then and tell her how splendid they look."

Daniel did not ask, "Will that be all?" Instead he inobtrusively walked out onto the front porch and just stood a moment. He flexed his stiff shoulders and relished the vast open space of the ranch yard. He was not a person for parlors and close places.

On the far side of the sprawling yard Chet grinned and waved. He and O'Toot were assigned to replacing some split sideboards on the cut-under wagon. With O'Toot it would have been a two-day job. Chet had the old boards prized off already.

Daniel wandered over by the summer kitchen.

"*Pssst.* Got a minute?" The whisper was so low Daniel barely understood it. Where was it coming from?

Wahoo's crutch wiggled over by the ocotillo fence. Daniel jogged over, knelt on hands and knees, and peeked through an open spot in the fence. "Wahoo! What are you doing back there?"

"Keeping an eye out for our thief, I hope. Need your help, if you have a little time."

"Glad to. What are we watching for?"

Wahoo pointed along the back of the house. "I borried your idea about baiting a trap. Used a pearl shirt button."

103

"For bait? Who'd want that?!"

"Dan, I'm sure Contrary was telling the truth when he said he didn't take those other things. He took a big wooden box full of paper, right?"

"What difference does that make?"

"Was it sparkly? Shiny? Small?"

"No, but—"

"Everything else that's missing is. Small and shiny. When you lost your bait, what was on the windowsill?"

"A brass wood screw." Things started to click. "A human thief wouldn't leave something in place of what he stole. A pack rat, Wahoo! Right?"

"Maybe. It would explain finding the silver sugar shell under a cabinet. The rat picked it up, then dropped it when he saw something he liked better."

"Of course. A trade rat. It collects shiny little things. Picks something up, finds something better and puts down the first thing. Why, if we find its nest, I bet we'll find the necklace and cuff links and even my gold piece." How simple the explanation was! Daniel stopped suddenly. "You look like something's wrong."

"Two pieces don't fit, Dan. When you're a detective, you gotta fit all the pieces right. Where did the pack rat get a wood screw?"

Daniel thought a moment. "On the workbench in the tool shed. I remember seeing them. And I remember hearing something

104

scurry once when I went in for some tools. No, for the cinches."

"But the shed's way over there on the far side of the yard."

"So?"

"They stick to a small area, Dan. They don't wander far and they don't like open space. A pack rat working around the house here isn't going to go clear across that big wide yard to the shed."

"Well, it seems he did. There was a wood screw on the windowsill. What's the other piece that doesn't fit?"

"The cuff links. A pack rat would only take one. But both are missing. Anyway, I have the button sitting on the ground below Mr. McGeehan's bedroom window. If there is a pack rat, we watch where he goes with the button and find his nest. But I have a blind spot over there. See where I mean?"

Daniel's eyes followed Wahoo's pointing finger. "If I sit by the gate on the far side of the house I could watch all the area you can't. We'd have the place covered."

"Go to it!" Wahoo paused. "Unless there's something else you have to do."

"I'm on my way." Daniel hopped up. "Y'know, Wahoo, this being a detective sure beats hanging curtains!"

Wahoo laughed and took a playful stab at tripping him as he ran off. Daniel crossed to the gate beyond the house. He settled himself under the mesquite by the gatepost and watched.

He realized very quickly how boring vigilance can be. He found his eyes, his thoughts, his attentions wandering. He must keep watch for a dusky tan little rodent that might flash for only a split second between the fence and the corner of the house.

Daniel scowled. Here was the Gladsinger, of all people. Why was he prowling around behind the house here, frightening off the pack rat? Now Daniel and Wahoo must wait a good while longer until the Gladsinger had gone and the rodent, wherever it was, summoned courage to move out into the open. The scowl faded. Daniel's mouth dropped open.

The Gladsinger paused by Mr. McGeehan's bedroom window, looking this way and that. He listened. He reached into his pocket. Sunlight caught on whatever he was taking out of his pocket and glinted brassy yellow. The Gladsinger thrust his arm with whatever-it-was in the open window and just as quickly yanked it back out. In his hand, silver glinted on a chain. He had just stolen Mr. McGeehan's pocket watch! Before Daniel could move or speak, the Gladsinger walked quickly around to the front of the house out of sight.

Daniel jumped the gate and ran along the back of the ocotillo fence, the shortest route to Wahoo. "Did you see that?"

Wahoo was struggling to his feet, swinging

106

his crutches in place. "I sure did! Run tell Mr. McGeehan. We gotta get that snipe before he has a chance to take the watch out of his pocket!"

Daniel ran around the corner and jumped the porch rail. He burst into the parlor at exactly the same moment Mr. McGeehan entered from the hallway.

The Irishman stood red with rage in the hall door. "Caroline!"

Carrie's head snapped around. "Sir?"

"Ye were out to the wagon fetching shears for the missus, were ye? Ye were strutting around back to steal me watch, that ye were! And ye leave this wood screw in its place. A joke, mayhap?"

Bridgid and Mom gasped in unison, no doubt the first time they had ever agreed on something.

"No, sir." Daniel took a step forward and stopped, cowed by the Irishman's fury. Even as he heard crutches clunking out on the porch, the Gladsinger entered the door behind him. "Sir, it was Galen here. I saw him take it."

"Liar!" Mr. McGeehan's face was the color of his hair.

"Now, just a fine minute, *Mr.* McGeehan!" Mom stepped forward quickly.

He turned on her with a wildly pointing finger. "Ye'll not bespeak me thus in me own house, madam! Nor shall this lad lie to protect his girl friend, accusing a God-fearing young man such as this in the bargain."

Wahoo clunked clumsily into the room. "I saw him, too, sir. Check this man's pockets, and you'll have your watch."

"And ye be the lad's chum. A clever bunch ye are, covering up for one another. Or perhaps, Dan, the thief be you y'rself. Ye had time and to spare."

The Gladsinger held his arms out wide. "Check my pockets, please, sir. We can put one story to rest immediately. Although I am certain Carrie could not have done such a thing any more than I could."

The brazen nerve of this fellow! Daniel admired the Gladsinger's marvelous gift of glib speech, even as the frustration welled up inside him. How easily the Gladsinger had talked Daniel out of being angry about that Contrary business.

The Irishman hesitated, then stepped up to the Gladsinger. He patted first one pocket, then another. Wahoo stood tri-cornered on his crutches, watching grimly.

Mr. McGeehan stepped back. "I didn't think so. And now we shall just as carefully search through the wagon out there, Mrs. Tremain."

"I object! The last time this—."

The Irishman withered her with his scowl. "And what might ye be hiding?" He charged forward out the door.

The women stood dumbstruck—all of them. Even Mom seemed to be without a thing to do or say. She put down her scissors and pushed between Wahoo and Daniel to follow Mr. McGeehan out. Wahoo and the Gladsinger locked eyes. The young Mr. Sanger turned on his heel and walked outside.

Daniel let Wahoo, slow as he was, go ahead of him. He did not want to even know what happened next. What if the Gladsinger had put the watch deliberately in the Tremain wagon? He had stashed it somewhere close. Surely not. The man had asked Carrie to marry him. A man does not do that kind of thing to a prospective wife, does he?

Carrie stood numbly by the porch post as Mr. McGeehan methodically ransacked the wagon.

Wahoo leaned forward and tapped her arm. "You give Galen an answer yet?"

"What?"

"He asked you to marry him, right?"

"Oh, that answer. What business is it of yours?"

"Please?" Wahoo studied her intently.

"I told him Pa was right, and I'm thinking I'm too young."

"In other words, no."

Why did Daniel feel so relieved? He could have jumped straight up and shouted for joy. But it was obviously not the time or place. He stood still, watching.

Wahoo lurched over to him, his mouth a thin, tight line. "You know, Dan, if he felt jilted, he just might stash it among her things for revenge—if he were angry enough."

Thoughts of joy faded.

Chet came wandering over, pretending mild interest. Daniel could tell how engrossed he really was, but then Daniel knew Chet better than did anyone else there.

Mom wrapped her arm around Carrie's shoulders, her face tight and bitter. Daniel noted that she would not look at the Gladsinger. She started to speak, licked her lips, and remained silent.

"Lose something?" Chet asked pleasantly.

"Mr. McGeehan thinks Carrie may have filched his pocket watch." Wahoo shifted uncomfortably. "Dan and I saw the Gladsinger snitch it. Now you know everything we do."

"Mm? Interesting. I saw Galen reaching down under the porch floor a couple minutes ago. That little rat run right over there." Chet leaned casually on the wagon.

Wahoo and Daniel looked at each other and took off running. Mr. McGeehan stood upright. Daniel was fastest. He jumped the rail and skidded over to the little hole under the porch where Chet had pointed. He tried to see inside, but it was much too dark back there, much too bright out here.

Chet reached for Wahoo's crutch. He brushed Daniel aside gently and wedged the crutch into the hole. He gave one mighty heave, and the porch floor board above the hole popped up. With a creak of nails and groan of wood he prized up a second board.

The nest contained a soft little cup of shredded cotton and a pile of debris only a rat could love. Black, shriveled peach pits, rusty horseshoe nails, and bits of harness leather studded the bottom. On top all sorts of glitter caught the sunlight—a silver spoon now tarnishing, two matching cuff links, pince-nez, a gold coin, an emerald tie tack, and the pearl necklace that had started it all. Here on the very top lay the watch and chain.

"Here's my five-dollar gold piece!" Daniel snatched it up.

"And how would ye know that?"

Daniel examined the coin carefully as he tilted it toward the sun. "I marked mine with two little notches cut exactly here. See?"

Mr. McGeehan took it to look for himself. "Where did ye lose it?"

"Wahoo and I both wanted to catch the thief. Independently, sort of. He was detecting; I was trapping. I laid it on the windowsill right over there, and when I checked it was gone. But a brass wood screw was there."

"Any wood screws in the nest, Dan?" Wahoo was peering down at an odd angle.

Daniel stirred through the cumulation of lovely and unlovely things. "No. No screws."

"Bet you'll find some in the Gladsinger's pocket."

"There were," Mr. McGeehan boomed. "As I

was checking his pockets I felt them. Didn't think a thing of it at the time—he's always making repairs about the place; 'tis natural he would have some."

Carrie stared blankly at the nest. "But why would he give the things he stole to the pack rat? Why did he put the watch in the hole?"

"It's a perfect place to hide loot," Daniel explained. "Even if someone sees him, there's nothing in his pockets, nothing in his bed or his room or his chest of drawers or anywhere. It's all here for a pack rat to take the blame."

Mr. McGeehan looked crushed. "There be no pack rat, not anymore. Upsetting Inez, it was, by coming into the summer kitchen. Frazier and I cornered it and killed it a couple weeks ago. I never woulda thought it of the lad. Never."

"I don't think he knew much about pack rats, though." Wahoo was staring again. "Or else he was taking a chance. A pack rat's just as likely to carry something out of its nest as it is to bring something in. The rat could have spread some valuable stuff around."

"And if it was found, more blame on the rat."

Daniel and Wahoo must have thought the same thing at the same time. Together they started to say, "Where is he?" when a horse clattered away out the far gate.

Wahoo shouted, "He didn't even stop to grab his hat!"

Chet yelled, "Untie 'm!" at Carrie as he bolted toward the wagon seat. Mr. McGeehan clambered up into the wagon, as Carrie yanked the tie line loose and Chet gathered in the lines. Mom's wagon lurched forward.

Daniel ran as hard as he could across the yard to the bunkhouse. Roller, at the bunkhouse hitch rail, stood with his head high and his ears doing wig-wags. The rattling wagon had disturbed his snooze. Daniel jerked the looped rein loose from the rail and threw it over Roller's head. He dragged the little horse's head around and pointed it in the direction of the gate. Roller was bucketing out the gate at a dead run by the time Daniel could pull himself up into the saddle.

Where had they gone? Daniel followed the faint dust cloud raised by the wagon, but within half a mile he had lost sight of it. He turned Roller aside and rode him to the top of a sloping ridge. He could see for miles from up there. And away out there, crossing the flat, were the Gladsinger and the wagon. Daniel watched, helpless, as the Gladsinger angled off onto a side road. The wagon dust continued on in what was now the wrong direction.

Daniel did not stop to think. He urged Roller up the brow of the steep ridge and sent him over the side with a whang in the ribs. Leaping, skidding, sliding, the little horse plunged down the bank. Loose dirt and stones rattled all around them. Then Roller evened out, stretching into a joyful, exhilarating run.

Daniel was not certain that the side road the Gladsinger had turned off on was the same road that lay on the other side of this hill. He could only pray it was. As in the fight, his own resources were not enough. And again, it rather surprised him that he remembered ahead of time to ask for help—in fact, to ask that God work things out His way.

Daniel climbed the hill up a broad and meandering wash. The wash grew narrower, steeper, brushier. On impulse Daniel dragged Roller's head aside and sent him up over the bulging hillside. As they crossed the flat hilltop and started down the far side, Daniel could hear no horse, see no dust or motion.

He came upon the abandoned road so suddenly he nearly rode right across it and on down the hill. He hauled Roller in, listening. Should he go up the road or down it? Was he behind the Gladsinger or ahead of him?

He was ahead! Daniel swung Roller around broadside to block the road as he listened to the beat of a single horse coming up the road. The Gladsinger came riding around the curve of the hill at a casual gallop. He hesitated, wide-eyed, and dragged his big-footed sorrel to a halt.

"Get aside, Dan!"

"I knocked Contrary down, and he's a lot tougher than you are."

If anyone knew that the Gladsinger did. He

glanced furtively down the hill behind them, up the brushy slope beside him. He seemed apprehensive about charging off cross-country. "I suppose you think you'll quietly lead me back to the ranch."

"Chet and Mr. McGeehan will be here in a minute. As soon as the Tubac road straightened out Chet could see you weren't up ahead. He's the best tracker in the world. He'll be here. Tell me why you did it. Weren't they paying you enough?"

He grimaced. "You're too little to understand."

"Try me."

"Very well. The greatest men in the Bible succumbed to temptation. Moses hitting the rock; David with Bathsheba and the matter of the census; Noah's drunkenness."

"So? That doesn't mean—."

"It *does*! If those great men couldn't stay on the straight path, how am I supposed to? There was a golden opportunity to get a little richer and blame it all on some pack rat. How could I hope to resist? It's not my fault, you see."

"Oh, yeah? I borrowed my Bible back from Wahoo and looked up some temptation stuff. It said in one place that we never get more temptation than we can handle, and that God always gives us a way out. Temptations are supposed to make you stronger, not crooked."

"Why am I sitting here arguing with a child? Get out of my way!"

Daniel heard the wagon coming in the distance. *Soon they'll be here.* "Try to get past me, and I'll bowl you right over the side. Tell me something. If Mr. Cadder and Mr. McGeehan had decided Carrie was the thief, what would you have done?"

"I wanted to marry her. I would have married her anyway, no matter what they accused her of. I—"

"But would you have spoken up?"

The wagon was close now. The Gladsinger glanced behind him down the road. He looked for a moment as though he would bolt. Then he turned his frightened eyes toward Daniel.

"I don't know." His voice was hoarse, almost a whisper. "I'm not sure I could bring myself to—I don't know."

Wahoo, sitting in the shade beside the summer kitchen, tossed his peeled potato into the big bowl. He reached for another potato. "What did I do to deserve this?"

O'Toot sniggered. He was trying to pare a potato as one would peel an apple—one long strand of paring. Potatoes do not lend themselves to that sort of paring; he was still on his first one.

"So what you do, O'Toot," Chet continued, "is ask God's forgiveness, see? Tell Him you're a sinner, and that you'll try not to sin any more.

Then you ask his Spirit to take over inside you. Take over your whole life."

"That's what *believe* means?"

"You already told me you believe Jesus died and rose from the grave."

"Yeah. Still—" O'Toot frowned. The curl of skin lay in an untidy little pile at his feet, the potato only half-peeled.

"In some ways it's real easy," Daniel chimed in, "and in other ways it's not. You see, if you—*oh, no!*"

A movement by the main house had caught his eye. Even as Daniel looked up, a dusky tan little rodent flashed across the porch, flicked its tail, and disappeared into the rat hole.